THE BLIND SWITCH

THE BLIND SWITCH

BY KELLEY SEWELL

MERACK PUBLISHING

Requests for permission to make copies of any part of the work should be mailed to the following address: info@kelleysewell.com.

www.kelleysewell.com

Published and distributed by Merack Publishing.

Library of Congress Control Number: 2017918946
Sewell, Kelley
The Blind Switch
ISBN 978-0-9996563-0-3

Text set in Georgia Regular

~

This book is dedicated to
Shawn Snyder, who has walked through fire
with me; and to our unstoppable sons,
Shawn and Cameron.

~

~

Acknowledgements

My heartfelt gratitude goes to the following individuals
without whom this book would not be possible:
To Mrs. B. and C., and the Marvelous Miss M. for providing
the kindling; to Russell and Christopher for knowing a
good hair-raising story; to Courtney for sharing my love
of the pen; to Sharon St. George for her inspiration and
encouragement; to Krista Clive-Smith, Susan Matthews
and Jimi Scherer for lighting my path; to Susan Barton
for reminding me that anything is possible; and to all
my family and friends whose love sustains me—
both those living and departed.

~

Chapter 1

Now that Mrs. Tanenbaum was pronounced dead, Mil Morgan, her legal counselor, was forced to find the key to her safety deposit box. He had been sifting far too long through a metal drawer of clients' keys he lugged into his private office from the back storeroom, anticipating the news that would set so many things into motion.

Morgan lamented how at one time he had organized his clients' keys by way of an ingenious fishing tackle system. One where he had carefully placed the labeled key to each client's safety deposit box in its own compartment of a dual tray jig box. Four jig boxes fit perfectly into a standard file cabinet drawer. This angling-inspired brainchild was just one of several peculiar manic endeavors Morgan had undertaken five years earlier in an attempt to cope with his younger brother's death.

Jamie's suicide was out of place, but Morgan knew that was only because he had lost touch with his brother. Although unaware at the time, in an act of compensation, Morgan immediately assigned a place to every item in his life he possibly could. From the canned foods aligned alphabetically in the pantry to the colorful textile cadre of shirts and pants standing at attention in his wardrobe, no matter how many times he got up in the middle of the night to check, he could breathe easy in the moment that they were still there.

His "extreme organization," as he fondly termed the condition in retrospect, drove him to the office when little else could. It forced him through his legal case files, leaving no slice of paper unturned. Legal documents belonged on the left side of the folder, correspondence on the right. Duplicates were immediately shredded. Sydney, his legal secretary bluntly asked if she was performing up to par. Morgan was too focused to notice her standing over him shaking her platinum blond head in exasperation. The last project had been this blasted key drawer.

As Morgan's grief, while never leaving him entirely, gradually faded into forced forgetfulness with a little help from a selective serotonin re-uptake inhibitor—aka Prozac—so did his drive to keep up his manic orderliness. As he took up fishing again, a pastime he had cherished with Jamie, he found he needed the tackle boxes for their manufactured purpose. Rather than buying new jig boxes like he should have, he simply tossed the keys into the drawer of the filing cabinet. Now he was paying for his lapse in organization. If only he could find the little silver key marked H. Tanenbaum.

Morgan closed his eyes and inhaled deeply. The image of Hildegard Tanenbaum's face came into clear focus. Hilde. Her electric blue eyes indelibly etched themselves in his mind. He could picture her smile; hear her soft, subdued laugh. The silver key with the typed label H. Tanenbaum found its way into his hand.

Morgan had less than ten minutes to make it to the savings and loan around the corner before it closed for the weekend. Once at the bank, in order to access the vault, he was required to show a copy of his driver's license to Nancy, a clerk that had waited on him for years and knew him by name. She seemed a bit miffed that he stepped up to her window just as she was closing out her drawer until he produced a copy of Hildegard Tanenbaum's Last Will and Testament.

"I'm very sorry for Ms. Tanenbaum's loss, Mil." Nancy pulled out the vault logbook with the pen attached and turned it so Morgan could sign his name. "I assume you'll be terminating the safety deposit box rental agreement today." He couldn't help but notice her glance at the large Roman numeral clock on the north wall.

"No, we will do that later as part of the estate settlement." Morgan replied.

Nancy's tall black heels did not impede her as she swiftly led Morgan to the vault. Once inside, she flipped through dozens of keys on a large ring to find the one that opened Drawer 667. She pulled out the metal box inside the drawer and handed it over to Morgan. She watched him as he carried the box to a counter-height stainless table bolted to the center of the vault floor. After a moment, Nancy told Morgan she'd be right back and that he only had a few minutes before the bank closed.

Morgan fished for the key in his pocket and quickly unlocked the box. It contained several documents plus a black velvet pouch. He set the papers aside for the moment and squeezed the soft pouch in his hand. He then turned it up on end. Out slid a dark green, crystallized teardrop that, by its size, must have been shed by the eye of a gargantuan creature. So, it did exist.

He carefully pinched the edges of the gemstone between his thumb and index finger and raised it briefly to the fluorescent ceiling light. It seemed to glow, but perhaps it was his imagination. The hair on his forearm lifted. The stone was much larger and more brilliant than he'd expected. Hilde had told him plenty of fantastical accounts he only half believed over the years he'd served as her attorney. Perhaps he shouldn't have dismissed her ramblings. Although he had been listed as a deputy on her safety deposit box rental agreement for years, Morgan never before had the inclination to inspect its contents. The existence of the Finian Star suggested validity to the elaborate stories Hilde had told over the years. This was the caliber of jewel people would risk losing their lives over. If Hilde had been truthful, a few lives had already been lost.

The clicking of Nancy's heels signaled that Morgan's time was up. He would have to review the documents and inspect the gem more closely at a later time. Fumbling, he rushed to push the stone back in its pouch and place the contents of the deposit box into his briefcase before Nancy reappeared with a deliberate downward glance at her Timex watch.

"I know, I'm out of time." Morgan sighed as he clicked the locks on the case and grabbed the handle. He nodded at Nancy indicating he was ready to exit the vault.

* * *

When Morgan re-entered his office building, he had already locked his briefcase in the trunk of his gold Mercedes sedan. Sydney had one hand buried deep within the bowels of the copier. Her other hand held back her waist-length hair from the aftermath of the black toner powder explosion that must have occurred while he was at the bank. Morgan hadn't paid a single maintenance bill in the five years Sydney Tracey had served as his secretary. She changed all the building's light bulbs and air filters religiously. She maintained all the office equipment and recently saved him a few hundred dollars by replacing the break room refrigerator condenser herself on a slow afternoon. Morgan knew Sydney was capable of so much more than her position at Morgan, Lipman & Jeter and wondered if she would ever figure it out.

Sydney's hand emerged from the copy machine covered in what looked like black soot, holding a scorched piece of paper. In contrast, her white linen suit and shiny platinum hair remained pristine. "There's the culprit," she smiled, releasing her blond river of hair, swaying it back in a Cher-like motion. Sydney was more than thirty years junior to Morgan. She was striking in an exotic way, with high cheekbones and flawless bronzy skin maintained with regular visits to the tanning salon.

"How did you do that?" Morgan shook his head in disbelief at her talent just before the headline of the day's local newspaper lying on the counter caught his attention. "State Horse Racing Board Investigates Diamond Head Stables." A lump formed in his throat.

"You got a hit on your ad," Sydney called in a loud voice as she made her way to the small employee-only restroom in an area behind the lobby counter to wash the black toner off her hands. The radio playing through the building was a sign that just the two of them were in the office. The radio was never played when clients were in the building. "A woman by the name of Ruby Sans called to make an appointment for Monday at ten thirty a.m. She has the coupon."

Morgan groaned. "Wasn't that a mistake? Make sure they don't run that ad again. I don't know why I let Kursta talk me into doing all these favors for her racehorse friends. I don't need any more business!"

"Hey, she's your girlfriend," Sydney laughed and hung her head out of the bathroom to continue the conversation as she washed her hands at the sink.

Morgan ignored the reminder and headed in Sydney's direction toward the "break room," an oversized closet with the door removed that stood across the hall from the restroom where Sydney was now drying her hands. He grabbed the first frosty glass bottle in a row of cola inside the oak antique icebox-style fridge and pulled up the bottles behind it to make the row straight again. He closed the door and popped off the cap with the bottle opener attached to the door.

A song came on the radio that grabbed Sydney's attention. "Do you know this song?" she pointed up in the direction of the speaker in the ceiling. It was part of an elaborate sound system that Morgan had since regretted investing in since he was focused on winding down his part of the practice.

"No, I don't know songs of your generation."

"Come on, Old Man, this song is more than ten years old." Sydney was more feisty than usual.

"Still too new." He took a swig of his soda.

"Listen to the lyrics," she coaxed Morgan. She started to sing. "Send me..." and then stopped. "What's Alaska's state flower?" she asked if she had suddenly turned into a game show host.

"Forget Me Nots!" Morgan lit up.

She sung the remainder of the lyric line, "...to help you to remember." She was definitely in a Friday mood. "See, there are little reminders of your retirement all around you if you just open your ears!" Sydney flashed him a bright white smile.

Morgan appreciated Sydney's playfulness. He admitted his retirement was all he could think of. He often caught himself daydreaming about the Alaskan sun rising over the horizon, the rose gold hues streaming across the sky, and the calls of ospreys. Once he settled his current clients' affairs, he could finalize his exit plan.

Her raising the subject created an opening he had been looking for. "I've been meaning to ask you, Sydney... what are your plans after I leave the firm? Are you interested in staying on when one of the other partners takes over this location? Or are you planning to do something different?" He could see that he put Sydney on the spot.

"Honestly, I'm not certain." She paused for a moment. "I thought about trying to get on with one of the local journals. I've been doing some freelancing lately."

"Hmmmm." Morgan nodded in acknowledgment and changed the subject. "What did you say was the name of my Monday morning client? Rita Sands?" He took a large swallow of his soda.

"Ruby Sans."

"Now, why does that name sound familiar?" Morgan muttered to himself as he turned away and headed in the direction of his private office with his bottle of pop. As he crossed the door threshold, he spotted a key lying on his desk. He stepped closer to his desk and saw that it was labeled H. Tanenbaum. He reached into his pants pocket and felt that the other one, identically labeled, was still there.

He pushed the intercom button on his phone. "Hey, Syd, did you put this Tanenbaum key on my desk?"

"Yeah, it was on the floor next to the drawer of keys you were going through. It must have fallen onto the floor. By the way, do you want me to reorganize that drawer for you? It's not good to have clients' keys..."

He didn't need the lecture. "Yes, please organize the keys."

"And don't forget... you have your Cardiologist appointment right before your first client Monday morning—at eight thirty a.m. sharp!"

Three months earlier, Morgan had suffered a heart attack and had been on blood thinners ever since. As a result, he would be required to have his blood coagulation checked on a regular basis for the remainder of his life. Sydney did a good job of reminding him of his appointments, but she certainly wasn't going to be following him to Alaska. If he had his way, neither would Kursta Blithey. He would have to devise another reminder system once he relocated to Anchorage; not just for his doctors appointments, but for many things. Whether it was stress, the byproduct of cardiac arrest, or his medication, his memory simply had not been serving him well. Just that morning, Sydney reminded him that he had forgotten to set the alarm the night before. It was the second time in two weeks. She stuck a Post-it note next to the front door with the word "ALARM" printed in block capitals, as if she were yelling at him on paper. Although Sydney had correlated the song on the radio earlier with the Alaskan state flower, Morgan couldn't help but wonder if she was trying to convey a more concerning message.

* * *

The rain found its way down the neck of Ruby Sans' trench coat as she fiddled with the front doorknob of her little blue rental house. She set her umbrella down to jimmy the wooden door open with both hands. "This is ridiculous!" She cursed not having an overhead porch roof. The last two days of rain had swollen the door shut. She shoved it as hard as she could with her right shoulder. The door flung open, sending her sliding across the entryway floor into the kitchen on her butt, shrieking as she knocked over a bucket half-filled with rainwater. She picked herself up only to slip again on the water-soaked hardwood floor.

Her landlords, Mr. and Mrs. Butts, seemed elated when Ruby turned in her rental application four years earlier. She'd decided to move to Tolstoy, CA at the prompting of her best friend, Suki. Ruby had just earned her Master of Science in Biology from a state university on the coast, and at the time, was ready to trade the coastal slog for the inland heat. The rare job offer as Butterfly Conservatory Manager at Tolstoy's animal exploration park and museum came up unexpectedly. Ruby knew she needed to jump on the opportunity and find a place to live—fast. She could have stayed with Suki for a few months, but preferred to avoid her boyfriend drama.

The Buttses didn't take the time to check Ruby's references or background. They just happily accepted her check on the spot for first and last month's rent along with a security deposit. Transplants from the East Coast, the Buttses had spent most of their lives in the little indigo house on Thine Avenue, but couldn't wait to rent it out so they could bask full time in the glory of a condo in the Sunshine State after Mr. Butts' retirement from the electric company.

"Mista Butts is real sick right now, Honey. He can't come out ta Californier and fix da sink," Mrs. Butts had explained to Ruby in her Jersey accent three years earlier when the kitchen sink clogged for the first time.

"I'm not asking Mr. Butts to come out to California. I

was just calling to let you know I will be calling a plumber to fix the sink, pay the bill and take it off my rent."

Ruby had subtracted many repairs off "da rent" and never heard anything from "da Buttses" until the day she placed seven blue buckets around her house to catch the rainwater. She received a certified letter from an attorney in St. Petersburg, Florida with an itemized invoice of past due partial rents and an eviction notice. She figured when it rained, it poured. She needed a lawyer. When she saw the ad for Milpeet Morgan, Esquire, she decided to give the man in the outdated black Resistol cowboy hat posing with his Airedale, "Weezer," a try. The ad came with a cutout coupon for a free consultation.

* * *

"Is something burning?" Ruby asked as she hung her raincoat on the brass coat tree in the warm waiting room of the downtown office of Morgan, Lipman & Jeter. The building was one of several charming craftsman style bungalows in the neighborhood that had been converted into offices about ten years earlier, in the eighties.

"Sorry for the smell. The coffee maker took a dive, but I got it working again. You must be Ms. Sans." The woman came out from behind the wainscoted counter to shake Ruby's hand. "I'm Sydney. We spoke on the phone."

Ruby looked down at the woman's hand streaked with coffee grounds.

"Sorry." Sydney quickly retracted her hand and brushed it off on her black rayon slacks.

Ruby laughed. "Call me Ruby." She looked at the grandfather clock in the corner. "I see I'm a bit early." It wasn't even ten o'clock yet.

"That's quite all right. Mr. Morgan is on his way and will be here shortly. Have a seat." She motioned to a dark leather couch facing two red plaid winged-back chairs. Ruby settled into one of them and leaned forward to thumb through the magazines, all issues of *American Racehorse* and *California Thoroughbred*, arranged neatly on the coffee table in front of her.

"Someone must be a racehorse enthusiast," Ruby said loudly enough for Sydney to hear behind the counter.

Sydney popped her head up. "Oh, yes. Mr. Morgan's significant other brings those in. She's big into horseracing."

A moment later, Mil Morgan entered the lobby from the back of the building, pulling a Band-Aid off the crook of his arm and tossing it into a wastebasket by the counter. He looked surprised when he looked up to see his first client already waiting in the lobby.

"You must be Ms. Sans." He walked over to her and extended his hand.

"Please call me Ruby." When she stood, her eyes were level with his. Since she had seen him pull off the Band-Aid with his right hand, she didn't want to shake it. She still did, but reluctantly and with a loose grip.

"Mil Morgan. Please," he motioned, "come back to my office."

An attractive woman with a full head of silvery hair and a tight black ribbed sweater that showed off her sculpted arms walked in to the office. She was holding a manila envelope.

"Margie!" Morgan lit up. He turned to Ruby. "Excuse me, just a moment." He left Ruby standing there to greet the silver fox. "What brings you in Margie?"

"It looks like the mailman got our two offices mixed up again," she laughed robustly. "It must be easy to confuse a shrink's office with a lawyer's." She handed him the envelope.

"Now, now!" Morgan pointed at her and gave her a smile with an extra spark. He took the envelope from her. "Thank you for the special delivery. You have a good day, Margie," Morgan said with a wink. He continued to smile as the woman exited the office. He turned to Ruby.

"Follow me."

Ruby followed the man's long strides down the hallway past a few closed doors. They stopped at the only one she could see open. The building was eerily still; nothing like the bustling law office she assumed it would be. Morgan motioned for Ruby to enter before him. She sat down in one of two black leather chairs facing the large mahogany desk.

In a silver frame facing her, Ruby immediately recognized the picture of Morgan and his dog from the newspaper ad. Next to it stood a photo of a strawberry-blond woman in pearls giving the viewer a provocative look over one of her bare shoulders. She was surrounded by a sea of black velvet that had faded into a hazy green along with the rest of her two dimensional world; no doubt, a product of sun exposure and neglect.

"I lost Weezer six months ago," Morgan shook his head and tightened his lips. "What a great hunting dog he was, my buddy. There's not a day that goes by that I don't miss him." He smiled at the picture for a moment and then turned his attention to Ruby. "What brings you in today?"

Ruby inhaled deeply, as if ready to give a speech. "I'm having problems with my landlords." She launched into the four-year history of her life in the small indigo colored house she called home on Thine Avenue, detailing all the repairs she had taken care of with no compensation. "I've been an excellent tenant. I have always paid my rent on time and I have cared for the house as if it were my own. Taking the cost of the repairs off the rent was my only course of action." She felt her face getting hot and took a deep breath. She had a hard time keeping her hands still in her lap. She ended with, "I'd like to know my rights," and took another long, slow breath.

Morgan stared at her blankly for a moment, and then suddenly turned his back to her to open a vertical file standing on the credenza behind him. "I'm listening," he said, although she had stopped talking. He pulled out a stapled document and started scanning the pages. When he got to the section he was apparently looking for, he set the document on the desk beside him and returned his attention to Ruby.

"Well, can they do that to me?" Ruby's expression of concern thinly veiled her curiosity with the paper distraction.

"Can who do what to you?" Morgan smiled, clueless.

"My landlords! Is it really so complicated? Aren't there laws protecting a tenant's rights?" Ruby felt the irritation bubbling up inside her. She folded her arms and pinched the inside of her bicep between her thumb and index finger, a habit that had stuck with her since childhood. "I'm sorry, is this not your area of expertise?"

"Ms. Sans, I don't mean to be rude. But, is there any other reason why you came to see me today?" Morgan glanced at the document he'd placed on the desk. He pushed the corner of the paper with his thumb to align it with the corner of his desk.

"You mean, other than my landlords?" Ruby couldn't help but wonder what the document was.

"That's right," Morgan nodded.

"No." She waited for an explanation.

"Ms. Sans, out of all the lawyers in this wicked little city, why would you happen to choose me?"

Ruby shook her head and closed her eyes at the question. With a sigh, she picked up her black faux alligator purse and began rummaging wildly through the contents until she extracted a folded piece of newspaper. She handed it to him. "I found your coupon in the paper for a free consultation. I thought you knew that. I told your secretary when I called." She wrinkled her nose. "I'll be honest with you. I can't afford an attorney, Mr. Morgan. I've never been sued or evicted. This is all quite unnerving for me." She took another deep breath. Her arm stung where she pinched herself.

Morgan softened. "Do you mind if I ask you a few

questions?" He picked up the document in one hand while reaching for his reading glasses with the other. The silence was palpable as he peered at Ruby over the top of his spectacles. "Do you have any family in the area?"

"Why?" Ruby's thermostat kicked on and she was suddenly compelled to lose her blazer. She wriggled out of it as Morgan continued.

"Is the name Tanenbaum familiar to you?"

Ruby set the navy blue blazer across her lap. "Yes. It was my mother's maiden name. Why?"

He turned his focus back to the paper. "Was your mother Laurel Alison Tanenbaum, Daughter of Elijah Tanenbaum, sister of Hildegard Adele Tanenbaum?" He peered back over the top of his glasses at her.

Ruby waited for a moment before responding. "Yes. Why are you asking me so many questions? How do you know so much about me?"

"Ms. Sans, I find it incredible that you have sought me out, because locating you was my major task for the week. Thank you for giving me the rest of the week off." He folded his hands and placed them on his desk.

"Why were you looking for me? I haven't done anything."

Morgan looked at Ruby curiously, cocking his head to one side. He turned the document to face her.

"'Last Will and Testament of Hildegard Adele Tanenbaum,'" Ruby read aloud.

"She was one of my dear clients. She passed away last week."

"Last week? She is—was my aunt. She raised me. I haven't seen her in years."

He nodded and pulled the document back slowly. "She was at Meadowview."

"Meadowview Convalescent? I live right around the corner from there." Ruby bit her bottom lip. "She was young to be in a facility. I'm thirty-three, so she must have been..."

"Seventy-two," Morgan did the math for her. "She had a stroke a couple of years back and couldn't take care of herself any longer." Morgan glanced down at the Will. "As I said, I'm looking for her sole living heir who happens to have the same name as you. Can I please see your ID?"

Ruby pulled her wallet out of her bag and flipped it open for Morgan to see her driver's license.

"Take it out and we'll make a copy."

"You said she passed away last week. Have arrangements been made?"

"There will be a rosary and visitation this Wednesday—day after tomorrow. The funeral mass will be Thursday."

Ruby found herself rambling as she was careful not to pull out a few credit cards along with her license. "I remember my Aunt Hilde had converted to Catholicism. I never knew what that meant, really. My mother just said that she gave up her family for Jesus... and the Pope."

"Are you Jewish?" Morgan asked.

She was a little surprised by the question, but then again, she brought up the subject. "Technically, I guess. I don't practice." She went silent.

Morgan pushed the intercom to ask Sydney to retrieve Ruby's license. In a matter of minutes, Sydney appeared, disappeared and reappeared again. She handed Ruby her original and the copy to Morgan.

"Hilde was smart about avoiding probate. You are the only person named in the will as a beneficiary. She listed you as the POD—Payable on Death beneficiary for her real estate and other assets, including a racehorse."

"A racehorse?" Ruby wanted to make sure she heard him correctly. "She actually owned... a racehorse? We had a horse on the ranch—a gelding name Beauty. I named him that after reading *Black Beauty* since that was my favorite book growing up. My Beauty wasn't black; he was a Paint. Sometimes I used to sneak into his paddock with a blanket at night and my aunt would find me there the next morning snoozing away." Ruby shifted in her chair. "I am surprised Hilde would own a racehorse so late in life."

"This was her second racehorse."

Owning two racehorses seemed out of character for Hilde, but who knew how she had changed over the years. "Really?"

"Your aunt had a soft spot for horses as well as people. I don't have to tell you how she was. She was your aunt after all. How did you lose touch with her?"

The question caught Ruby off guard and she couldn't stop the hot springs that poured from her eyes. "She sold my horse without telling me. It's a long story, but without me having to pay you for a psychotherapy visit as well, the short version is that I was young and immature and held a grudge."

"I'm sorry," Morgan immediately grabbed a box of tissue from his bottom desk drawer and put it where Ruby could reach it in front of the woman in the green photo. "It's none of my business. Do you want to talk about your landlords?"

Ruby took a tissue from the box and blew her nose. She shook her head. "I do, but considering what I've just learned, I need a little time."

"Of course." Morgan grabbed one of his business cards from the holder on his desk and handed it to her.

Ruby glanced at the card briefly and slipped it into her purse. "So, did she have another stroke? What happened to her?"

Morgan looked down at his desk and seemed to struggle with what to say next. "She had congestive heart failure but they are not sure why she ended up going into kidney failure." Morgan cleared his throat and turned the pages in Hilde's Will so that the first page was on top again.

"What do you mean they are not sure?"

He locked eyes with Ruby. "They are conducting an investigation."

"An investigation?" Ruby ran her fingers through

the crown of her dark, wavy hair. "Mr. Morgan, are you suggesting that my aunt did not die of natural causes?"

Chapter 2

It took a while for Ruby to pull herself together after her meeting with Mil Morgan. Losing her aunt Hilde was bad enough without a lingering question about the cause of her death. Morgan had explained that a medical error was being investigated. There had been some question about whether she had been receiving the right dose of Furosemide for her congestive heart failure. The investigation into her death up to this point was clinical and not yet criminal.

Ruby returned to her little blue rental in far worse condition than when she had left that morning. At least opening the door didn't require as much shoulder strength this time. She accepted that she would have to put her legal battle with the Buttses aside until after Hilde's funeral services were concluded.

Planning ahead for Wednesday and Thursday, she decided to call into work to give her boss a heads up that she would need to take another two days off that week to attend her aunt's rosary and funeral masses. While he appreciated her not waiting to tell him until she returned to the museum, he did inform her that she would have to find her own coverage for those two days; and reminded her about the second grade class that was scheduled to visit on Wednesday.

Although it was the middle of the day, Ruby decided to take a hot bath as a way to encourage a nap before reporting to the club where she would be performing that evening.

Ruby supplemented her income and fed her creative side by singing in jazz and blues clubs for the last few years. As a girl, she sang in the choir all through school, and also at home with her aunt. She hardly felt like singing after her trip to the lawyer's office, but hoped that a bit of rest would transform her, as it usually did.

She turned the chrome faucets in opposite directions and sprinkled some bath salts into the tub as she waited for the water to get hot. Once the water was high enough, she eased herself into the tub that wasn't quite long enough to contain her legs. Every time she rested her heels on the ledge, she told herself she'd have a longer tub in her next house.

Ruby played back some of the conversation with Mil Morgan in her head. Admittedly, the question about how she had lost touch with her aunt was something she was not prepared for. She had locked many of her childhood memories in a box, which she then submerged in some dark swamp at the back of her mind.

As a teenager, Ruby had spent more time with her aunt than her mother. Hilde referred to Ruby's mother as a "live wire", but Ruby chalked her up to what she really was—an unfit parent. Ruby's father didn't say much about Ruby's mother and wasn't around much himself. He was the region's busiest farrier and traveled from ranch to ranch shoeing horses. When he came home one day to find Ruby's mother gone, he blamed himself for not spending enough time at the house—but he didn't change his behavior. Hilde became the ground in Ruby's charged adolescence.

Ruby bent her knees to allow her upper body to slide completely into the bath water. She sunk her head so that only her nose was exposed for breathing. She opened her eyes and gazed for a moment at the blurred ceiling above her through the lens of the water. Her eyes stung so she couldn't keep them open for long. She closed them again, but remained just under the surface of the tub water as she breathed comfortably through her nose. Suddenly, a memory bubbled up.

Ruby was in high school and had been living with Hilde in her farmhouse when Ruby's mother showed up after a "long trip" lasting more than a year. The evening her mother arrived, Ruby was getting ready to perform in the school talent show. She wore a dark green, strapless satin dress with a parachute skirt that Hilde had sewn for her. They were just locking up the house to leave for the school when out of nowhere, Ruby's mother's beat-up, green Chevy Nova showed up, dispersing a brown cloud of gloom and doom in the gravel driveway. Ruby and Hilde's eyes locked. Hilde had a look in her eyes that assured Ruby that she knew how important this night was for both of them, and that she would be damned if anyone was going to ruin it.

Over the years, Ruby observed that her aunt had sharpened her skills in dealing with her sister's insatiable need for attention. Ruby was afraid those skills would be put to the test that evening.

"Grainger!" Hilde ran to her sister as the woman exited the car and slammed the door. Hilde gave her an extra long hug; probably so her sister wouldn't question whether she was truly happy to see her. Ruby's mother's real name was Laurel but had always insisted on being called Grainger—even by her own daughter. She said it was sophisticated and reflected her personality better than her birth name.

"What a surprise!" Hilde gave her sister an extra wide smile and then pulled back to get a better look at her. "You doing OK?" Hilde asked. Ruby tried to sense the mood her mother was in and gauge whether she had been drinking or taking pills.

"Fine, I'm fine!" Grainger flipped her long dark hair and stepped away from her sister. "I'm here to pick up my girl," she announced in a big, bold voice, as if she was staking her claim; as if she had rehearsed the line in the car on the way there; as if other people were listening.

Ruby stood frozen on the front steps, wishing her mother would melt away if only she could find a bucket of water to throw on her.

"Aren't you going to come over here and give your mother a hug?" Grainger forced a little laughter into her words, as if that would make the idea more inviting.

Not putting up a fight, Ruby stepped quickly but carefully down the wooden stairs, in the green heels that Hilde had dyed to match her dress. She crossed the gravel drive on her tip toes over to her mother to avoid getting them too dusty. She gave her mom a polite hug. "We were just headed to the school. I'm singing in the talent show."

Grainger acted as if she hadn't heard a word Ruby said and stepped back to get a better look at her, holding both of her daughter's hands out as if they might dance. "Well, aren't you a vision in that dress," she gawked.

"Auntie Hilde made it for me," Ruby beamed.

"Of course she did." There was no disguising the edge in Grainger's tone, but she tried to make up for it. "It's beautiful. You're beautiful."

Ruby's anxiety was mounting. "I have to be at the school at six thirty. We really need to leave now." She felt as if the lining of her stomach was starting to dissolve. She pinched her bicep with her index and thumbnail until it hurt.

"I guess I'm not as important as the Butte Valley High School talent show." The edge returned in Grainger's voice.

"Nonsense," Hilde quickly chimed in, as if she'd known her sister would say that. "Ruby rehearsed her song for two months and I've spent a week getting the bodice to fit right, given her recent growth spurt. She's nearly moved up a full cup size in the last month."

"Was that really necessary?" Ruby asked.

"My point is," Hilde continued, "this is an important night for Ruby."

Ruby wanted to fall into a hole in the ground.

"Come with us, Grainger!" Hilde blurted out, patting her sister on the back.

Ruby couldn't believe her ears. Did she really just say that? Hilde shot her a quick wink. It took a second, but Ruby caught it and knew to play along.

"Yes... Mom. I worked really hard on the song. Wouldn't you like to see me perform it?"

"I'm not really dressed for a talent show." Grainger looked down at her cropped khaki pants and not-so-white Keds. "Maybe I could borrow a blazer?" she turned to Hilde.

"Your jean jacket is adorable. Look, I'm wearing jeans. Only the kids who are performing are dressing up." Hilde reasoned.

"What are you singing?" Grainger asked Ruby. Ruby wondered why it should matter, but answered her mother. "It's a Carly Simon song."

"I love Carly Simon!" Grainger clapped her hands together in glee.

Ruby and Hilde exchanged eye smiles, keeping their secret.

"Do you think we could sing it together?" Grainger asked.

"It's a high school talent show, Grainger," Hilde reminded her. "It's for the kids. I'll tell you what, when we come back to the house, we'll all sing some songs together. Like old times." Singing and music had always been part of the Tanenbaum family. Hilde played piano most of the time and sang the accompanying parts. Since Grainger had been out of the picture, Ruby was singing the lead more than ever.

"Well, do you really want me to go, Ruby? Because if you don't want me to, I won't."

"No, Mom, I really want you to come—more than anything, and it wouldn't be half as much fun if you weren't there." Ruby pinched herself at the lie. "This is like a dream—you showing up when you did. Like it was meant to be."

Grainger paused and looked at Ruby for a moment. Her lip began to quiver and her eyes became shiny. "It is, isn't it?" Not missing a beat, she piped, "Well let's go then. We don't want you to be late!" She climbed into the front seat of Hilde's pale blue Mercury. Ruby took her place in the backseat.

"You know, I went to Butte Valley, too." Obviously, Grainger had forgotten whom she was talking to, as if Ruby and Hilde were acquaintances instead of family. "I was in the glee club."

"Remember, we were in the glee club together?" Hilde reminded her.

"Oh, yes, but you were in the B Choir. I was in the A."

Ruby knew Hilde wouldn't deny Grainger her claim to fame. Ruby wondered where her mom had wandered off to this time, but wouldn't dare ask. Her mother pulled her hair so that it rested over the front of her right shoulder, exposing the back of her neck. Ruby spotted the top portion of a new tattoo her mother must have gotten since she had seen her last. It peeked out above the collar of her jean jacket like the tip of an iceberg just below her hairline.

The whole two miles from the house to the school, Ruby prayed she could get through the performance without her mother causing a disturbance; however, as they pulled into the school parking lot, her trepidation transformed into a private, smug confidence. Lined up on the sidewalk of the school were kids holding up signs reading, "Ruby Tanenbaum, our choice for Talent Queen!" "We love you, Ruby!" "Ruby is SOLID GOLD!" Ruby thought Suki, her best friend, and a few other friends might be there to greet her, but she had no idea there would be so many.

"Well, Ruby, it looks like you have yourself a little fan club." Her mother's tone couldn't hide her blush of envy.

As she thought about the melody and the words she would sing, Ruby decided that what she had said to her mother back at the house was actually true. Her mother being there was meant to be, and she was going to sing her heart out to her.

Hilde pulled up to the front of the school. A flock of kids ran over to the car. Grainger started to open her door but Hilde put her arm out in front of Grainger. "We will be parking the car. This is Ruby's moment." Grainger took her hand off the door handle.

Ruby opened the car door to her friends chanting, "Ruby! Ruby! Ruby! Ruby!" Scott Walters, Ruby's recent crush stepped up in a navy pinstriped suit and offered his arm. "May I escort you in?" Ruby closed the car door and looked back at Hilde with wide-eyed excitement. She pinched herself in the arm again, but it didn't hurt this time. She grabbed Scott's sleeve confidently as the car pulled away.

Ruby was the last act. She wondered if her mom would be able to sit through the Jonas Juggling Twins, Hilary the Hula Hooper, and the seven other performances before hers. From her seat backstage, she spotted her aunt and her mom seated in the center of the front row.

But when Ruby walked onto the stage, her mother's seat was empty. She hadn't seen her leave. The audience began chanting Ruby's name.

Ruby stepped up to the mic. "How are you all doing tonight?" The crowd cheered wildly in response. "There is someone very special in the audience. Some of you know my Aunt Hilde, who sews some of our costumes for the cheer squad and the glee club."

The audience cheered again. Some kid from the back yelled, "Yo, Hilde!" and another one whistled. Grainger caught Ruby's eye as Grainger made her way back down the aisle to her seat. Ruby looked down at her mother and smiled.

"And, there's someone I haven't seen in a while who's with us this evening, as well." The gym grew quiet. "My mom." The crowd cheered again loudly. "We both have always loved this song that I'm about ready to sing to you right now, and I'd like to dedicate it to her."

The music started and Ruby could see that Grainger immediately recognized the song.

"*You're So Vain*?! I love that song!" When it came time for the chorus, Grainger stood up along with the rest of the crowd and sang loudly, "You're so vain! You probably think this song is about you!"

Ruby sang for her mother and to her mother. She felt powerful within the safety of the lyrics. At the same time, she saw the pride in her mom's eyes as she gazed up and sang back to her. It was a strange connection, but it was still a connection.

* * *

Ruby heard a voice yelling and jolted upright into a sitting position in the bathtub.

"Oh my God, you scared me to death! I thought you were dead." Suki, her roommate, had pulled back the shower curtain and was staring down at Ruby naked in the water. "Did you fall asleep? I was calling you from the living room. I heard the dripping of the tub faucet. Sorry to barge in on you." Suki was visibly distraught and had been prone to being jumpy given recent events. "Don't you know how dangerous it is for you to be under the water like that if you fell asleep? What are you doing in the bathtub in the middle of the day, anyway?" Suki turned to pull some toilet paper off the roll hanging next to the toilet and blotted underneath her eyes.

Ruby was a bit disoriented. "I'm sorry. I wasn't asleep, just in deep thought. What time is it?"

"Two thirty. What time do you have to be at the club?"

"Five for a Five thirty opening set. I was going to take a nap, but I'm pretty awake now. Would you mind handing me a towel?" Ruby pulled the plug from the drain.

"So, what's the story with the attorney? Are we going to have to move?" Suki handed her a soft gray towel. Ruby proceeded to dry herself off.

Ruby understood it was natural for Suki to want to know what was going on with the landlords, but she disliked the question suggesting they were a package deal. Ruby was more than willing to have her closest friend stay long enough to get back on her feet after the violent break up with her boyfriend, Armando Lewis—a crazy prizefighter that used Suki as a punching bag one night and nearly strangled her to death. However, Ruby had hoped Suki was preparing to find a permanent home. There was no denying that Suki was a good roommate. She was fun to be around, paid her portion of the rent on time, and always left the place clean. It was her post-traumatic quirks that tried Ruby's patience, like her habit of sleeping on Ruby's bedroom floor and getting up half a dozen times in the middle of the night to make sure the front door was locked. Plus, it made Ruby nervous to think about the Buttses having more ammunition against her if they found out that Suki had been staying beyond the consecutive three-day timeframe allowed for guests in the lease.

"My conversation with the lawyer got a bit... sidetracked." Ruby wrapped the towel around herself and tucked one of the ends between her breasts to keep it in place. She reached for the blow dryer, wishing Suki would give her some space.

"What do you mean?" Suki took a step back.

Ruby didn't want to rehash the details. "It's a long story, but I found out my aunt died and the attorney I went to happens to be the executor of her will."

"Oh, not Hilde." Suki frowned. "She was more like a mom to you. It's so sad that you didn't get to say goodbye."

The words stung. "Tell me about it. I'm ridden with guilt. She was at Meadowview Convalescent. There's a question whether someone at the nursing home made a mistake and gave her too much of her heart medication."

"That's horrible. You mean, like... killed her?" Suki

backed towards the door to give Ruby more room.

"I don't know what it means," Ruby shook her head. "I have a few hours before I need to be at the club. I think I'll go over to Meadowview before I have to get ready to go to the club and see what I can find out." She flipped on the blow dryer, hoping Suki would get the hint that she wanted the bathroom to herself.

* * *

Meadowview Convalescent had built a positive reputation as a posh place to put one's aging parents. However, as soon as you pushed the glass door open, you'd swear the commercials were describing another place. A pungent concoction of urine, bleach, and canned vegetables hung about the air.

Ruby forced herself to continue down the hallway. To think that Hilde lived there was almost unbearable. Chins lifted from chests like helium balloons floating to the ceiling as she passed by. Grimaces, smiles, and blank expressions locked onto her face and followed her as she made her way down the long, railed corridor. She stopped in front of a small black woman with bleached-blond hair who was wearing a pink pinafore and mopping the floor.

"Excuse me, can you tell me which room Hildegard Tanenbaum was in? She passed away last week."

"Thirteen B." The woman looked up at Ruby with an unusual interest. "They are preparing the room for someone else."

Ruby thanked the woman and proceeded down the hallway.

"Are you a relative?" the woman called to her in afterthought.

Ruby ignored her and continued on until she saw the number she was looking for at the very end of the corridor on the right. There were two beds in the room and they were both made neatly. A woman in purple scrubs was emptying the contents of a dresser drawer into a plastic garbage sack. She turned to look at Ruby.

"May I help you?"

"I'm Ruby Sans. Hildegard Tanenbaum was my aunt."

The woman smiled. "I'm sorry for your loss. I'm cleaning out her drawers right now, and I wasn't sure what to do with her belongings." As the woman swept out the dresser with a hand broom, Ruby went over to the bedside table where a few pictures stood in frames. One of the pictures in a green wooden frame caught Ruby's attention, and she bent down to get a closer look at it.

"That's a precious picture, isn't it?" the woman asked. "Hilde always talked about that little girl. No one could ever figure out who she was, and every time we asked her, she had a different answer. One time it was her neighbor's child, then another time it was her niece. She never had any children of her own; none that anyone knows of anyway. Do you know who it is?"

The picture was of Hilde when her hair was long, dark, and wavy. She stood with her arms around a little girl whose eyes took up the top half of her face and a smile that was almost as wide as her jaw, revealing a lost front tooth. Ruby immediately recognized the little girl as her six-year-old self. The woman was right with either answer about the little girl. Not only was Ruby Hilde's niece; she and her parents lived next door for a time in the small two-bedroom house on the same property as Hilde's farmhouse. In the picture, Ruby and Hilde stood on Hilde's porch steps. Both houses were surrounded on three sides by an almond orchard. Hilde always called them "ammands."

The woman turned around to take a better look at Ruby. "That little girl is you!"

Ruby smiled in agony. She picked up the picture and held it in both hands. She was swept back to that faraway place where the creek water numbed her ankles as she waded through the stream behind the orchard with Hilde.

Sometimes they would ride Beauty together across the creek if the water was up too high. The scent of the almond blossoms permeated the screen of the back summer porch as they drifted into sleepiness on their matching cots on warm nights.

Ruby noticed the picture behind that one. It was of a dark racehorse covered in a blanket of Black-Eyed Susans, his jockey atop the saddle with a cheesy winning smile. She did not recognize the horse, but it made her think of Beauty.

"That was her first racehorse, Kingston. Wasn't he beautiful? He won the Preakness. Hilde just loved him. His death was so tragic."

"What happened?"

The woman's voice got a little quieter. "He collapsed in his stall after a race here at Diamond Head racetrack. They never said what caused it. Did you see in last week's newspaper that the State is investigating Diamond Head Stables?"

Ruby shook her head no. "Why?"

"I don't really follow horse racing. I'm too busy working, but I have heard rumors over the years that some funny business goes on there."

"What do you mean?"

"I don't know. Illegal activities. Like I said, I don't know much about it. It's a world of it's own. Hilde had hoped to breed Kingston. She ended up getting another racehorse after he died. I think her attorney talked her into it. He visited her a lot. He was the only one that came to visit."

The words cut deeply.

"We all loved Hilde dearly. She was especially close to Elsa, the Director." The woman pulled a tissue out of her pocket and cleaned her glasses hanging on a chain around her neck. "I tell you, as much as you see death around here, you'd think you'd get used to it. But, when you have a resident like Hilde who loved both people and animals with an overflowing heart... well, you don't." Her eyes reflected the yellow light from the ceiling. She smiled. "Would you like to keep the pictures?"

Ruby nodded her head yes and crossed her arms. She dug her nails into the underside of her arm as she thought of what she would say next. "I understand there are some questionable circumstances around my aunt's death."

The woman looked at her in surprise.

"What? I don't know anything about that. You'll want to talk to Elsa the Director. I know she had Congestive Heart Failure for a long time, but there isn't anything particularly questionable about that." The woman was not alarmed in the least bit, which was odd to Ruby. Perhaps she was being truthful and really didn't know anything about it.

The woman placed the pictures in the white plastic sack sitting against the wall with Hilde's other belongings. "Did she ever tell you about her trip to Africa?"

Ruby's breath caught at the woman's words and her nails made their way deeper into the softness of her inner bicep. "No," she calmly responded, "I was supposed to go on that trip." The image of the African map she used to hang on her bedroom wall in Hilde's farmhouse came to mind. She had pushed seven of her aunt's mix colored pearl-top sewing pins into the spots on the map they had planned to visit together. Ruby had taken the map and the seven pins with her when she moved out. She still had them tucked away in a box somewhere. She promised herself long ago in high school that she would go to Africa some day, even if not with her aunt.

"Why didn't you go?"

Ruby thought for a moment as she searched for the right words. "It's a long story, but I ran away before we were supposed to go on the trip. I had a falling out with her and my mother, and when I came back, she was gone. I realize now that she had to go on the trip with or without me, but it was devastating. She sold my horse as there was no one to take care of him, and I never forgave her.

"Well, it was probably a good thing you didn't go. She told everyone she lived there for a while, next to a diamond mine. She said the man she married over there was killed... in the mine."

"He was actually killed?" Ruby remembered a picture that Hilde kept on her bedside table of her exotic beau, Nuhr Dhanuka. Ruby could not forget how Hilde sparkled when she talked about him. He was a far cry from the farmers and mechanics that made up the male gene pool in their small town.

"That's what Hilde said. Murdered over a diamond. Not just any diamond, but one that changed colors."

"Really?" Ruby swallowed.

"Well, that's what she said. She had a wild imagination. She was the best storyteller I ever heard." The woman took a cloth and wiped down the front of the dresser.

"Did you believe her?" Ruby asked intently.

The woman looked around as if to check if anyone was listening. "I loved Hilde dearly, but between you and me, I think she was, well... a little off her rocker."

Ruby was a little put off by the woman's comment, but admittedly, she was right about Hilde's storytelling talent. Ruby remembered many bedtime stories of faraway places and intriguing characters that had kept her begging her aunt for more.

The woman reached for the garbage bag leaning against the wall. You should take this stuff. If you don't, I'll have to throw it out. It's clothes and books, mostly."

"OK," Ruby put her arm out to take the bag.

"Oh dear, you must have been stung by a bee or is that a spider bite on your arm?" The woman drew attention to Ruby's self-inflicted welt.

"It's nothing," Ruby forced a smile and put her arm down to her side, tightening her grip on the white plastic bag.

"Can I ask you a question?" The woman leaned against

the dresser. "Why are you here... now? I don't mean to be nosey. It's just... we tried for years to locate Hilde's relatives. We could never track anyone down."

Ruby didn't answer but was able to dig her thumbnail into one of the fingers wrapped around the bag.

"It's none of my business, I guess." The woman looked down at the floor for a moment and then returned her gaze to Ruby. "Her rosary is on Wednesday and the funeral is the day after. Are you going to the funeral?"

"Possibly," Ruby mustered up the best response she could while her head swirled in a vortex of unanswered questions.

"Well, if you'll excuse me, I need to get some cleaning supplies. It was nice meeting you. You said your name is Ruby? I'm Agnes." The woman closed the dresser drawers and left the room.

Ruby let out a huge exhale, not realizing she had been holding her breath. She glanced at the window and walked over to get a better view. From behind the mulberry trees, she could make out the roof of her own little blue house. She wondered if Hilde had ever seen it.

"Hello." Ruby heard a different woman's voice behind her—a sharp voice—with a German or Austrian accent.

Ruby turned around. A tall woman with a grave face and tightly pulled back red hair held a hand out to Ruby. "I'm Elsa Tetonke, Executive Director of Meadowview. And who might you be?" A tight-lipped smile pushed over the woman's mouth. Ruby knew she was trouble.

"Ruby Sans. Hilde was..." Ruby could tell by the woman's expression that it didn't matter who she was.

"We do accept visitors. However, since you have no one to visit, you are loitering."

Ruby was unnerved by the woman's tone but returned her words calmly. "You don't understand. I loved my aunt very much and I feel terrible that I lost touch with her."

The woman wouldn't listen. "Let me tell you what I do understand. I understand that I held your aunt's hand as she expelled her last breath with no family around; that she never had any family around for the entire time she was in my care—only an attorney with less than honorable intentions."

"Are you referring to the suspicious circumstances around her death?" Ruby's heart pounded as she asked the question.

"What are you talking about?" The woman furled her brow.

"Didn't Hilde take Furosemide? Isn't that a medication for Congestive Heart Failure?" Ruby asked, knowing only what Mil Morgan had told her.

"I cannot discuss patient confidential information with you. You are not authorized. And that attorney of hers shouldn't have been authorized either. He shouldn't have had access to her accounts or to her assets. He had the keys to her estate. He didn't keep it maintained but he certainly collected the maintenance fee every month. He talked her into terrible decisions for his own financial gain. Who talks a client into buying part of a racehorse when she's in a long term care facility, for God's sake?"

Ruby didn't know what to say, but she wanted to know more.

The woman paused for a moment before continuing "And as for you... I find it interesting that you show up right after your aunt passes away, like a vulture. You have no business being here now. It's too late. You have two minutes to say goodbye to this empty room before I have security escort you out." The woman turned and left the room.

Ruby grabbed the sack, and looked for a rear exit out of the building. They were all marked as emergency exits with alarms. She was convinced that although Agnes said she could take Hilde's belongings, that nasty administrator certainly wouldn't approve. Ruby had no choice but to press the white plastic bag to her side and hide it with her purse as she made a beeline for the front doors. She looked down at the linoleum floor to be as inconspicuous as possible and walked as fast as she could toward the entrance.

Ruby heaved a sigh of relief as she reached the automatic glass doors. As the doors opened, the Director suddenly appeared from outside the building. She was coming back in! Although Ruby wanted to flip her the bird, she did her best to give the woman a big smile, hoping it would distract her from looking down at the bag.

"Have a good day!" Ruby chirped, which turned the woman's scowl into a look of surprise. Ruby turned the corner in wonderment that she got away. Luckily, her car was the closest, just beyond the handicapped space. She ran to it, slipped behind the wheel with her bags, and pulled out of the parking lot as fast as she could.

Ruby had just enough time to get home and get ready for her gig at the club. She placed the picture of her and Hilde on the coffee table facing the sofa and put the sack with the other picture as well as her aunt's other items in her bedroom. Suki bartended at the same club most nights of the week, but her shift started at four. Ruby squeezed herself into a dark red velvet dress with spaghetti straps, strapped on some black patent mary janes, fluffed her hair and spread on some red lipstick before heading out with her raincoat in hand.

Chapter 3

Three Months Earlier

Julian Kleptstein was the proud owner of Clobert's, the premier jewelry company owned by his family for generations, located in the center of the city. Since he was a boy, his dream had been to own the business outright. This dream was now a reality, with the recent establishment of his father's irrevocable trust. His father was in ill health and had stepped down as CEO six months prior. Julian had plans to launch a media campaign, sponsor community events, and most importantly, create a world-renowned gemology institute. Clobert's employed and contracted with the industry's leading gemologists, jewelry designers, and appraisers. Kleptstein himself had earned a reputation as one of the nation's finest gemologists, and Clobert's had become synonymous with not only world-class designs, but also the highest level of customer service.

In contrast, Kleptstein's personal life was in complete disarray. He longed more than anything to be in love. He lay awake many nights wondering what it was about him that repelled women so much. He wasn't a bad-looking guy and took extra steps in his self-care. He started waxing his back after a few people commented on his "sweater" during his recent vacation in Hawaii; and he was working out in his home gym at least five nights per week. He was getting pretty solid.

He was also reading all the right books on relationships. He had just started *Men Are From Mars, Women Are From Venus*, a book that was released the year before and gaining in popularity. He had also taken some cooking classes, and was game for making a meal for the right special lady. He couldn't understand why women he was interested in would never accept a second date with him. He discussed it at length with his psychiatrist, Dr. Margie Fox.

Kleptstein had been seeing Margie Fox for years to help him with his obsessive-compulsive disorder (OCD), which centered on women in recent years. Although he had never committed any crime, he acknowledged he had stalker-ish tendencies. Once he developed a fancy for a woman, he wanted to know everything about her, down to the tiniest of details. He longed to follow her home to see where she lived; to imagine what she looked like asleep in her bed; to know her bathing habits. He couldn't bring himself to tell Dr. Margie that sometimes he followed women home to their houses.

He and Margie talked about coping mechanisms to keep his OCD in check. He even came up with his own strategy of giving the woman of his desire a rose or multiple roses to show his affection and to remind himself that he was to behave like a gentleman. Only gentlemen with manners and sophistication gave roses. The roses reminded himself of the type of man he wanted to be. Margie told him she thought it was a brilliant scheme, as long as it did not make the object of his affection feel uncomfortable.

* * *

It had been an especially long afternoon in the showroom after a tenuous morning spent with the city over building permits for the institute. Rain had been coming down in sheets for the last few hours accompanied by regular cracks of thunder. There had been few customers. No one wanted to brave the mess outside.

Kleptstein decided to lock up at 5 p.m., a rarity these days. Deciding to face the weather armed with his black umbrella, he shuffled his way through the dark Orange Street tunnel, which was beginning to collect water in the center, across Harbinger Avenue, and up the narrow stairs to Curiocity Sushi and Blues, a funky sushi restaurant by day, and a swanky blues club by night. He had developed a recent habit of frequenting the place after locking up the shop. He was there at least three nights a week, but usually arrived a few hours later.

As he got close to the top of the steps, he could hear the familiar blend of tones from the Curiocity house band. It was a comforting sound, a sound to count on. No matter what had happened during his day, nor what worries troubled his soul at night, Curiocity was there to make his world right again. He could pick out Charlie's lilted mood on the piano and Harvey's struggling fingers on the bass (he'd only been playing a few months). Of course, Rif kept it all together with his soft brush on the snare drum, "tititty tat, tititty tat."

But, something was different this afternoon. As the toe of Kleptstein's shoe touched the top step, a note must have escaped an angel's mouth. The sweetest, silkiest voice he had never heard before softly kissed his ears and sharply penetrated a place that could have only been his heart. Kleptstein would have sworn he had died and wafted up to heaven. But as he looked to the stage, he saw that rather an angel had fallen and graced with her presence the little wooden platform at Curiocity Sushi and Blues.

The voice came from the most near-to-perfect creature Kleptstein's eyes had ever savored. The woman was rather tall—he guessed about five foot nine—with just the right amount of skinny. Her dark, minky hair cascaded around her shoulders like a waterfall he'd like to swan dive into, and her magnetic, sable-brown eyes drew him in as if he were a moth ready to meet its fate in the flame.

Visually intoxicated, he managed to make his way up to Chai, the M.C., who was leaning against the bar. "Who's the Seraph?" Kleptstein asked.

"Hmm?" Chai clearly didn't understand him.

"The angel, on the stage."

"Ruby Sans. What a voice, huh? Vin sure got lucky this time." Vin booked the gigs at the club. "This place has never been so slammed, and it's only five thirty."

"Where did he find her?" Kleptstein asked while keeping his focus on the woman center stage.

"She was working over at Monroe's. They stiffed her on three months' pay, so she came and sang for Vin. He booked her on the spot."

"Of course he did." Kleptstein motioned to the petite bartender with pink hair and a dynamite derrière. "Sloe gin fizz." He ordered his drink while conjuring a way to connect with the unapproachable creature on the stage. He leaned over so Chai could hear him. "He better keep this one." Chai gave him a thumbs-up in agreement.

As the next song started, a clap of thunder coincided with a flash of lightning, shutting off the power. The room went pitch black and the sound was gone. Kleptstein thought this could be his chance to find the angel vocalist and be the hero to help her out of the building. The room went silent for a moment, and then people started talking as they realized the power might not be coming back on anytime soon.

There was a lot of commotion between the bar and the stage. People were speaking loudly and pushing as they made their way to the entrance that doubled as the exit. As Kleptstein pushed through the crowd, he realized he was swimming upstream. The current of people was headed toward him. By the time he got to the stage, Ruby was gone. He sat on the edge of the stage in the darkness and waited for the crowd to ebb away.

Kleptstein finally made his way down the stairs and

out of the building to find his car, which was parked behind the club. As he turned into the alley, he spotted Ruby in a black trench coat up ahead. She opened the door to her car—a black 1974 Karmann Ghia coupe. She turned to look in his direction before getting in and speeding off into the darkness.

* * *

One Tuesday evening, after watching her faithfully every week for three months, Kleptstein got the nerve to approach Ruby between sets with a dozen ruby red roses. She seemed overwhelmed, or maybe impressed. She thanked him and kept saying how beautiful the roses were.

Although Kleptstein had no problems talking to people under normal circumstances, he wasn't sure what to say to someone who affected every fiber of his being. While he conjured up the conversation he really wanted to have in his head, he spewed out a cheap secondary dialogue of compliments and comments on their common musical tastes. His mouth embellished his secular achievements at the jewelry institute while his heart attributed Ruby as his reason for believing in a higher being. He silently ascribed her every gesture to Divine inspiration while he told her he liked the way she rolled her r's and l's, common to the style of Celtic singers. She laughed politely in warm tones with wide eyes and opaque expressions; and after much persuasion, agreed to have a drink with him "someday". She had to cut the conversation short, as it was time to start the band's final set of the evening.

Kleptstein was electrified. Ruby had said yes to a drink. That was technically a date. He clung on to each note of every song she sang for the next hour. The set was almost over as soon as it started.

Kleptstein knew it was against his better judgment when he decided to follow Ruby home that night. It was two thirty in the morning, and though he should have just gone home, he felt compelled to know where she lived. So, he waited in the alley behind the club until she left the building and got into her car. He then quickly ran to start his maroon Chevy Impala, which was parked around the corner, and trailed her at a comfortable distance to her home. He pulled up to the apartment building next door to her house just as she entered and closed the door behind her.

At this point, he was dumbfounded. What was he to do from here? Knock on her door at quarter to three in the morning? There was nothing else to do but pull the car around and go home. Then, out of nowhere, Ruby suddenly appeared at the window, as if she had heard his thoughts, and set a burning candle in a glass votive cup on the windowsill. For a moment, her face glowed in the light. Kleptstein ducked down in the seat while gazing up at her glorious visage. He hoped she wouldn't see him. As quickly as she had appeared, she vanished again. He watched the candle flicker and imagined her silhouetted form in the light, envying the sheets caressing her every curve as she turned over in the night.

* * *

As the sun emerged the next morning, Kleptstein woke up a bit chilled and stiff-necked in the front seat of his car—just in time to see Ruby leave her house in a tight, fitted black suit, matching scarf around her face, and dark glasses. She paused briefly to adjust her snug skirt at his driver's side window; not noticing him crouched in a ball in the corner of the white Naugahyde seat. She moved on to her little coupe, got in, and pulled away from the curb.

Once again, the voice of reason told Kleptstein to go home, but he failed to listen. After all, where could Ruby be going on a Tuesday morning dressed like a vocational vixen? She didn't say anything about a daytime job. Kleptstein knew he should go home, take a shower and get to the showroom. There was a lot to be done with the week's shipment coming in, and he was expecting a new client. Mike, the General Manager, would be there to open, but Kleptstein was also meeting with the design institute architects. Kleptstein deliberated only briefly as to how he would justify his late arrival. He was the boss, right? He shouldn't have to justify anything.

In the spirit of the previous evening, Kleptstein started his engine and traced Ruby over the river bridge, past the historical park, through the middle of town to the west side (she was driving awfully fast), and up a hill to the parking lot of the Saint Mary's Church of the Immaculate Conception. At one point, Ruby looked in her rearview at a stoplight. Kleptstein was sure she had seen him. Ruby swung her car into an open spot, open and slammed her car door, and ran with small steps in her heels to the entrance of the church. A hearse parked in front announced a funeral service. Kleptstein parked his car and, followed Ruby at a casual pace, adjusting his collar.

His heart was pounding. He shouldn't be there. How would he explain himself? A second thought suddenly came to him and provided an immediate sense of calm. He had come this far and knew a lot of people in town. Chances were, he even knew the deceased. Throwing all caution aside, Kleptstein pulled open the heavy wooden door and proceeded inside.

A little woman with blue hair and poorly fitting dentures handed Kleptstein a prayer card for Hildegard Adele Tanenbaum. He accepted it with a polite smile, walked down the center aisle, and took a seat two rows behind his beloved Ruby.

There were five people in the church, and one of them was a woman seated in his row with red hair pulled into a tight bun. Kleptstein looked over at her. Their eyes met briefly. He smiled at her but she just looked at him as if he had no right to be there. He returned his focus to the back of Ruby's long, slender neck, where it remained for the next twenty minutes as the rosary was recited.

At the conclusion of the mass, the small group in attendance filed up to view the casket. Ruby rose slowly from her pew. Kleptstein and the woman in his row followed behind. Kleptstein noticed Ruby was a bit wobbly and her shoulders were shaking as she approached the casket. Clearly, Hildegard Tanenbaum was someone that meant a great deal to her. A pang of guilt caught Kleptstein for being there in the church.

As the line got closer to the casket, Kleptstein found himself literally inches behind Ruby. Her fruity perfume was intoxicating. He longed to bury his face in her freshly washed hair. He noticed she was sobbing quietly, her whole body trembling. He wanted to comfort her, to reach out and touch her shoulder, but he knew that would be crossing a line.

Suddenly, Ruby turned around to face Kleptstein, but she did not see him. Her eyes fluttered back in her head and her body swayed like a wispy willow. Kleptstein had no choice but to catch her in his arms as she passed out cold.

* * *

Ruby opened her eyes to see the vaulted ceiling above revolving slowly. The stained-glass patterns turned inward, overlapping each other as if she were looking through a kaleidoscope.

"Ruby? Are you OK?" Blurry faces hovered over her in a circle. She felt hard wood beneath her and realized she was lying on a pew in the church.

"Did I pass out?" Ruby asked. She recognized Morgan's face.

"Yes. Can you sit up? We have some water here for you." Morgan held a Styrofoam cup in one hand.

Ruby pushed herself up into a sitting position with the

help of Morgan and Kleptstein. Her arms were still shaky.

Morgan held the cup up to Ruby and helped guide it to her mouth. She took a sip.

"Are you feeling better?" Kleptstein asked her.

Ruby's eyes came into focus. Ignoring the question, she looked toward the far end of the church. "The casket is closed. I didn't get to see her."

"Do you really want to see her?"

Ruby turned her face in slow motion toward Morgan, who repeated the question. "Do you really want to see her?"

Ruby's eyes filled with tears. "Yes. Why would they close up the casket so quickly? I'm her only relative. I should get to see her."

"Of course you should. We'll have the Funeral Director open it up again." Morgan went to find the Funeral Director while Kleptstein kept watch over Ruby.

Ruby turned to Kleptstein. "What are you doing here? Did you know Hilde?"

Kleptstein swallowed hard and squeezed his eyebrows together in a look of concern. "Yes, as a matter of fact, I did." He did not elaborate, but rather changed the subject. "I own Clobert's here in town."

"Yes, you told me last night. Hilde was my favorite aunt, but I hadn't seen her for a long time. I didn't even get a chance to say goodbye. I just found out—under very strange circumstances—that she passed away." There was a drop in conversation.

"I'm very sorry for your loss..." Kleptstein looked down at his shoes and noticed he had paper stuck to the bottom of one.

Ruby directed her attention to the front of the church where the coffin was being re-opened. Morgan quickly returned to Ruby.

"Are you OK?" Morgan asked.

Ruby nodded and set the finished cup of water on the pew next to her with a shaky hand.

"Let's get you to your feet." Morgan took the lead and held one of Ruby's arms, while Kleptstein took the other. "There you are. We will walk with you."

Ruby's heart raced and she saw little white spots again as she got closer to the casket. She had that same disconnected feeling that she did right before she passed out. "Give me a second," she whispered.

"Of course," Morgan responded.

They stopped. Ruby took a couple of deep breaths. "I want to see her, but it's been so long. How could I let my foolishness keep me away from my favorite aunt? She was like a mother to me. How can I ever forgive myself?"

"Don't do this to yourself," Morgan consoled her. "She loved you. She told me. She only had love for you." Kleptstein held onto Ruby's other arm in silence.

She turned to Morgan. She looked directly into his eyes. "Swear to me that she told you that."

Morgan nodded.

"I need to know. The guilt I have is unbearable." Ruby was having a hard time controlling her breath, she was crying so hard.

"You need to catch your breath," Kleptstein said to her quietly.

Ruby looked at Morgan intently. "She said that?"

Morgan met her gaze. "Yes, she said she only had love for you."

Ruby needed to hear that in the moment. It didn't matter if it was true. She had to hear it and she had to believe it. "I'm ready." She breathed in staccato. "To see her."

As they drew closer to the casket, Ruby could see her aunt's ashy, wavy hair from the side. It was no longer the dark chestnut she had remembered, even if she had colored it at the time. Ruby saw that she was wearing a dark blue suit.

Morgan and Kleptstein held Ruby by the arms, steadying her as she reached the opening of the casket. Her eyes settled on her aunt's face. She turned and frowned at Morgan. "This is not my aunt."

Morgan looked at Ruby with raised eyebrows. "What do you mean?"

Ruby burst into a full hysterical wail. "This is my mother!"

Chapter 4

The Funeral Director calmly, but briskly, walked up to the casket to see what the matter was.

"This is Grainger Tanenbaum. Her real name was Laurel. Laurel Tanenbaum. This is not Hildegard Adele Tanenbaum. This is not my aunt. It's my mother."

Morgan and the Funeral Director looked at each other in confusion. Elsa must have overheard what Ruby said, as she now approached the casket. Ruby turned to her. "Is this the patient you had in your facility?" Ruby's shakiness was now gone and replaced with an aggravated resolve.

"Yes, of course, this is Hilde."

"You have the wrong person here. Let me see the death certificate," Ruby demanded.

"I'll have to go back to the car to get it," the Funeral Director said flatly and headed out of the church. Kleptstein took the opportunity to excuse himself as well. Ruby barely noticed him leave.

"I haven't seen my mother or my aunt in many years, but I know who each one is and what they look like. This is my mother." Ruby's eyes started welling with tears. "You—all of you—need to straighten this out. And, now I need to know what happened not only to my aunt, but to my mother as well."

The Funeral Director came back with the death certificate and handed it to Ruby. It was Hilde's. Ruby noticed the primary cause of death was Congestive Heart Failure and Kidney Failure was the second cause. The

Funeral Director excused himself and said he was going to make a phone call. He came back a few minutes later.

"I am so sorry, Ma'am. There has been a mistake. There is another funeral scheduled this afternoon at the Jewish synagogue across town. That is where Laurel Tanenbaum's service will be held."

"This is Hilde, I am sure of it!" Elsa insisted.

"Elsa is right. This woman is Hilde." Morgan echoed. Ruby figured this was the only time Elsa and Morgan had agreed upon anything, but they were both wrong.

"Obviously, neither of you knew that Hilde was an identical twin." Ruby sighed incredulously. "Just how well did you know her?"

Elsa and Morgan looked at each other in disbelief.

Morgan pressed, "Even if she was a twin, how do you know this isn't her?"

"I honestly can't believe you are questioning me about the identity of my own mother, but just to indulge both of you, let me ask you a question. Did my aunt ever tell you the story of when she was bitten by a rattlesnake as a kid?"

Morgan shook his head no.

Elsa's eyes lit up. "I do remember that story, and she had a nasty scar from the venom on her left forearm. I've seen it myself."

Ruby reached over and pushed up the sleeve of the woman in the casket. There was no scar.

Elsa raised her eyebrows and sucked in her breath just a little.

Morgan looked at the Funeral Director. "What are you going to do about this?"

* * *

Morgan insisted on driving Ruby to the funeral home where both bodies were to be delivered and placed in their proper resting vesicles. Ruby had lots of questions about her aunt's finances and his management of them that she wanted to ask Morgan, but like her landlord issues, they would have to wait. She had more pressing questions that needed answers. When had her mother died, and how? Was her death related to Hilde's? Did they stay in touch? All signs seemed to point to their estrangement. All Morgan could tell her is that her mother was omitted from her aunt's will. Whether it was intentional or not, he did not know.

Ruby felt a hole in her chest. Ruby didn't know if she would ever be able to forgive herself for allowing the pain of her adolescence to separate her from her two mothers—the one who brought her into this world and the other who shaped it around her. She had created a life without them, and now she was paying for it. She would do anything to bring them back, even the mother who had abandoned her and could never love anyone as much as she loved herself. *These are childish thoughts*, she told herself as she climbed the mortuary steps with Morgan guiding her by the arm.

"Don't worry, we'll get this all straightened out." Morgan patted her shoulder awkwardly.

Ruby knew there would never be any straightening out of anything, but she vowed as her last act of love to them, that she would see to it that each woman was correctly identified and laid to rest according to her wishes.

As soon as Ruby and Morgan entered the mortuary lobby, the Funeral Director was ready to usher them back to a small viewing room. As he led them down the dimly lit, wood-paneled hallway, he apologized incessantly to Ruby for the "mix-up." He kept repeating that "this" had never happened before, like that mattered. She figured it was necessary on his part, but it was still annoying.

"I still don't know how my mother died. Was her death related to my aunt's?" Ruby asked the Funeral Director as they continued down the hall.

"Laurel died of a heart attack on Monday. I'm not aware of any connection." He frowned, as if he knew his response would be disappointing to Ruby.

He then directed them to a small room with the two caskets open and each one positioned against the opposite wall. There was just enough room for a narrow aisle between them. Hilde lay in the pine box in a white hooded linen garment. Ruby didn't need to look at the scar, but to prove to Morgan, she pushed up the white linen sleeve and pointed it out to him.

He nodded in acknowledgment. "Seeing them side-by-side, I can tell them apart."

Ruby studied the women's faces and hands, the only parts of them showing, for signs revealing details about their lives since she had last seen them. Her mother's face had more lines and grooves, a product of smoking, excessive drinking, and over all lack of self-care, no doubt. Hilde's face, in contrast, was puffy like a marshmallow moon—likely a sign of her chronic congestive heart failure.

Ruby noticed the rosary beads in her mother's hand and reached into the casket to pull them out. As soon as she did, the Funeral Director swooped in to help, as if she might mess something up or discover the hidden apparatus holding the hands together in perfect position.

"Here, let me..." He removed the string of beads and turned to the other casket to place them into Hilde's hands in the pine box. "We understand Hildegard was Catholic and Laurel was Jewish," the Funeral Director acknowledged. "Let me assure you that Laurel was not embalmed. We had only put her make up on. We can remove it. We will change their clothes and caskets, and then Laurel's service will be this afternoon at two o'clock. She will be buried immediately afterwards, according to Jewish tradition. Hildegard's funeral mass will be held tomorrow."

"But Hilde didn't have a rosary." Ruby reminded him. "My mother had a rosary. And don't bother removing her makeup. She'd prefer to keep it on, believe me."

"I will call the church and see if they can hold

Hildegard's rosary at four p.m."

Ruby thanked him and calmly informed him that she would wait in the lobby until the bodies were switched, and then come back in to expect them. Morgan stepped outside to make a few phone calls. About thirty minutes later the exchange was completed, and Ruby could move on to the next steps of burying her mother and seeing to it that her aunt was given her proper rosary. So many services in one day.

* * *

Through the window of Morgan's sedan, Ruby watched the white bubbly cumulus clouds sit on an invisible plate over the eastern part of the city. He wheeled her back to the church to pick up her car. He had been kind enough to drive her through a fast food restaurant first so she could eat a little something before Grainger's service, but she wasn't hungry. As he pulled up to her car, which was now the only one in the lot, he asked if she was feeling better.

"I'm numb," she responded.

"Please eat a couple bites of that sandwich, at least." Ruby had not yet opened the wrapper. "I won't be there to catch you if you faint again. Does that happen often?"

"No, it's never happened before, but today has been full of 'first times,' if you know what I mean." She did her best to give him a smile. He nodded as she opened her passenger door to get out of the vehicle. "Thank you for the ride."

"Don't mention it." Morgan returned the smile. Before Ruby could close the door, he remarked, "I hope you don't mind me asking, but do you know that man that caught you when you fainted? The one that helped me get you to your feet?"

Ruby had to think for a moment and nodded. "He is a regular customer at the club I sing at. I was surprised to see him. He said he knew Hilde, but didn't say how."

"Would you consider him a friend?"

"A friend?" Ruby raised her eyebrows. "Hardly. Why?"

"He seemed awfully concerned about you in the church. We all were, but when you were lying on the pew, he stroked your hair in a way that..."

Ruby's eyes widened and her body shuddered. "He stroked my hair?"

Morgan nodded.

"In a way that...?"

"In a way that suggested he..." Morgan didn't finish the sentence.

A shiver shot through Ruby from the bottom of her feet, up through the back of her legs, and into her stomach.

"Something about that guy is off. An attractive young woman like yourself can't be too cautious."

Ruby nodded. "Right. Thank you." She looked down at her watch. She needed to go. She said goodbye to Morgan. As his car pulled out of the parking lot, her skin creeped at the thought of Julian Kleptstein touching her while she was unconscious. She scanned her surroundings before stepping into her little black sports car.

* * *

Ruby pulled into an open space in the side parking lot of the Congregation Beth Israel. There were about twenty cars; more than she expected. As she rounded the corner toward the entrance of the synagogue on foot, her heart sped up as she noticed a line of Harley Davidson motorcycles in front of the building. Just who was her mother? A Hell's Angel?

Ruby held her breath for a beat as she entered the foyer. An older woman donning a smart black tailored suit with perfectly coiffed hair resembling a silver helmet made her approach.

"Are you family?" she asked.

Ruby nodded her head.

"Follow me. Are you Laurel's daughter?" The woman turned her entire upper half when she addressed Ruby, as if there was some problem with her neck preventing her from turning her head. She did not introduce herself and Ruby was fine with not making the acquaintance of another new person for the remainder of the day.

The woman showed her to a room where the family was to wait for the service to begin. Ruby would have been all alone had it not been for a man in a dark blue suit sitting with his back toward the door on the far side of the room. She didn't spot him at first. His jacket and pants were close to the same color of the chair he was sitting in. As Ruby got closer to him, she could see that he was bent over with his head resting in his hand. He must have heard Ruby and turned to face her. His eyes looked like he had been crying. They were red and swollen. He quickly stood and pulled down on the bottom of his suit jacket, which seemed a bit snug for him. He must have been about six foot four and a solid two-fifty. Ruby guessed him to be close to fifty.

"I'm sorry, I didn't hear you come in the room." He held his hand out to her. "I'm Travis. You must be Ruby?" So much for not meeting another person.

"Yes." She shook his hand. Ruby racked her brain, trying to figure out who this guy was. She didn't have any cousins on her mom's side, as Hilde was her mom's only sibling and didn't have any children.

"You don't know who I am, do you?" He raised one eyebrow.

Ruby shook her head. "No, I'm sorry, I don't. However, I assume we might be related since we are in the family waiting room."

"I know this is a strange place for us to meet, but uh, I'm your brother. Technically, half-brother." Ruby knew anything could happen when she walked into the building, but she couldn't have seen this coming.

"This day has been full of surprises." She took a deep

breath to take it all in. "So, you're my brother." What else was there to do but give him a hug? She extended her arms out to the friendly giant. When he bent down so that she could reach him, she started to sob.

He patted her back. "It's OK. I've been a mess myself. Let it out."

After a few moments, Ruby pulled away from him and grabbed a tissue from a box sitting on a small table in the corner along with a pitcher of water and some clear plastic cups. "Would you like some water?" she asked. She poured herself a plastic cup full and downed it all in three long swallows.

"I'm good, thanks." He paused briefly. "I was adopted. Grainger..."

Ruby cut him off with a laugh. "Ha, yeah, you must be my brother. What kind of parent makes her kid call her by her first name?"

"I know, right?" Travis shook his head and continued. "It was really strange how I met her..." Travis stopped talking and turned his attention to the Rabbi who entered the room.

The Rabbi was friendly and soft-spoken. He greeted them and said a blessing and a prayer in Hebrew. Ruby didn't understand the words, but she could feel the power in them. The Rabbi handed her and Travis a black torn ribbon to pin on the left (heart) side of their clothing and they were guided to their seats in the first rows of the Congregation.

"Mom was in a motorcycle gang?" Ruby whispered to Travis as they sat down.

"Motorcycle club," he corrected her.

Ruby couldn't wait to talk to Travis more and to hear the story of how he reunited with Grainger after being adopted. Ruby figured their mom must have been nineteen or twenty when she had given Travis up for adoption.

After the service, everyone drove to the cemetery for a brief graveside service. Ruby stayed just until it was over and then rushed off to attend the real rosary for Hilde before her final service the following day.

Chapter 5

With Hilde Tanenbaum's service and burial behind him, Morgan was anxious to get back to the bank to unlock the second H. Tanenbaum deposit box. It was Friday and his afternoon calendar was clear. In repeat fashion of the previous Friday, he showed Nancy his ID and signed the logbook. He noticed she was much friendlier this time, even asking about his plans for the weekend. Then again, it was only 2 p.m.

She handed him Box 696 this time. He took it to the metal table and set his briefcase alongside it. He turned the key in the lock and the box opened right up. Nancy stood against the doorjamb and waited. With his back turned slightly to her, he inspected the contents. There was no paperwork this time, just a blue velvet drawstring pouch much like the black one in the first deposit box.

He quickly turned the pouch upside down and loosened the cinch. Out slid a green stone that appeared identical to the one back at home in his office safe. He could not understand why Hilde would keep the stones in separate boxes at the bank. He was certain only one stone was mentioned in her will. He looked forward to going home where he could compare the two stones more thoroughly in private. He opened his briefcase to place the blue pouch inside, and locked it up. He let Nancy know he was ready to go.

* * *

Morgan's shiny Mercedes 500 SEL swerved on autopilot up the windy road to his hilltop haven ten miles north of town. As he passed the equestrian sign, Morgan knew he would be pulling into his driveway in just six-tenths of a mile.

The single door to his three-car garage closed like a protective hand behind his sedan. With his briefcase in hand, Morgan entered his ranch-style home through the utility room, where an automatic sensor light came on. A series of lights came on without the touch of a button as he turned into the hallway, and then into the study. It didn't matter that it was the middle of the day. A black safe stood in the corner. He turned the built-in combination lock—right, left, then right again. Once open, he plucked the black velvet pouch from the safe, which also housed his handguns and their corresponding ammunition, and took it over to his desk.

He opened the black velvet pouch and let the stone slip onto the black leather blotter topping his desk. He opened his briefcase and pulled out the blue velvet pouch. He opened it up and set the stone beside the other one.

Morgan clicked on his very bright desk light to get a better look and took a seat. The stones looked the same. He took one in each hand. Identical. He held each one to the bright light and rotated them in his hands. There was no difference in how they reflected the light. He set them down on the desk, side by side, and pulled out a copy of Hildegard Tanenbaum's will from his briefcase. He had read it dozens of times before and knew there was no reference to a second stone, but he read it again anyway. His index finger traced each word in haste. He knew the document was not going to give him an answer. As he reached the last line, he resigned that there was nothing else to do but take the stones to a jewelry store in the morning to be appraised. For all he knew, one may be a fake. The radio had been playing ads about the revitalized Clobert's jewelry mart and its associated gem institute under construction. He decided he would take the stones there.

The phone rang in the kitchen. He wondered who would be calling him at home in the afternoon. He figured it was probably a sales call, but decided he'd try to answer it before it went to the answering machine. He picked up the handset mounted on the wall by the kitchen cabinets just before the fourth ring.

"Hello."

"Hello, I can't wait to see what you're making me for dinner tonight." It was Kursta.

Morgan froze. He suddenly remembered that he had told her a few weeks ago while they were making up after a fight that he would make her dinner for their twentieth anniversary. He had completely forgotten that it was tonight.

"Does six o'clock still work for you?" Kursta asked.

"Umm, yeah, but six-thirty would be better."

"I'll see you then."

Morgan made a call to Sydney, who, luckily, was still at the office.

"I'll take care of it," Sydney chirped on the other end of the phone. "It's a good thing you caught me, I was just setting the office alarm on my way out. The usual from Chez Jeanty, right? Coq au Vin times deux?" This was not the first time Sydney had ordered dinner on Morgan's behalf from Kursta's favorite restaurant.

"No, Steak Diane for me."

"If you get two different entrées, she'll know you didn't make it."

"Fine, fine—two Coqs au Vin. She's going to know I didn't make it anyway. And get two mousses au chocolat."

"Got it. Did you get her a card?"

"Aaagh, no."

"No gift?"

"I did get her a gift, but it isn't ready for pick up yet."

"Really? What did you get her?"

"A new vacuum from Sears," Morgan said sarcastically.

"You didn't get her a gift either, did you?"

"I've been busy."

"I'll pick her up a card and a pair of tasteful, but not too expensive, diamond earrings from Macy's."

"And get yourself something too. Keep yours under fifty."

"Done." Sydney hung up.

Morgan looked at his sink full of dishes and the white tile countertop still displaying the aftermath of his attempt at making homemade Bolognese sauce a few night before. It looked like a bloody crime scene. If he was really going to make a go at fooling Kursta into believing he made Coq au Vin, he'd better get to work. The only reason he felt inclined to go to such great lengths was that this was the last anniversary he planned on spending with Kursta Blithey.

Looking back, Morgan could hardly believe he had been with Kursta for twenty years. Not all the years were a waste. There were specific things that drew him to her in the beginning, like her wildly hypnotic French accent and her soft, thin frame. She had the quintessential French feminine look, complete with a finely defined nose and lips that looked ready to kiss every time she formed a consonant. There was a time when he simply could not resist what he coined her "cabaret charm."

Kursta was well connected in the community and well versed in local politics. A first-generation French-American, she served as a city councilmember for four years early in their relationship. They met during her campaign at a fundraising mixer. Morgan acknowledged that Kursta was responsible for most of his business referrals over the years. That used to be a good thing.

What Morgan had savored most about his early relationship with Kursta was that it didn't interfere with the mechanics of his life. He could be physically intimate and socially active with an attractive and intelligent woman who didn't question his actions or scrutinize his motives. Kursta used to be content with accompanying him to social functions and lectures, sitting quietly by a fire with a glass of brandy, and debating the latest local political scandal. She was fiery and passionate yet knew her place. She knew when to leave him alone and when to attend to his physical needs. She didn't threaten his freedom by twisting him into some sort of emotional or financial commitment. All those qualities he had cherished in Kursta and because of them had harbored fond feelings for her.

At one point, Morgan considered cohabiting with Kursta. He remembered the evening he almost asked her to move in with him. They were sitting in a canoe smack dab in middle of the little lake on the ten-acre stretch behind his house as the sun began to set. Kursta had been sleeping over almost every night for the last several months, and being together just seemed right. They faced each other with their knees touching like a couple of kids, eating the grapes and cheese he had packed for them. The final rays of the days' sun cast a glow around Kursta's face that made him almost want to cry. He leaned over and gave her a very long, lingering kiss. Her lips tasted sweet from the red seedless and her breath smelled like his favorite Vermont cheddar. That was the moment he was going to ask her, but some little voice in the back of his head said, *Not yet*.

Later that week, Jamie pulled the plug on himself and nothing was ever the same again. There was no doubt that Kursta carried Morgan through some of the darkest days of his life; but slowly over time, their relationship atrophied. Morgan blamed Kursta because she was the one who changed. The independent and autonomous woman he once adored became static—as in cling and white noise. She talked incessantly about "where they were going," as if their relationship was a destination. Worst of all, she kept bringing up his retirement and only wanted to talk about finances.

Kursta had developed unhealthy spending habits. Every social function and horseracing event called for a new outfit. Kursta didn't bring in much money as the General Manager of Diamond Head Stables. Somehow, over the years, she had developed an unspoken expectation that Morgan's job was to subsidize her credit card debt and her bad horse deals.

Morgan acknowledged his part in enabling Kursta's behavior, but that was all about to change. It was his time to enjoy life. He had worked long enough, building the law firm into four branches in the north part of the state. He didn't need new clients. He took on the last three to help out one of Kursta's friends at a local independent newspaper in need of some ad sales. Ruby Sans was the last new client he intended to take on, and it was really as a final favor to his former client, Hildegard Tanenbaum. He was ready to begin a new chapter in his life, and it was to start with him finding a new home somewhere in the outskirts of Anchorage.

Chapter 6

Kursta herself had grown weary of her "dealings" with Morgan, but she wasn't ready to write him off entirely. He had served as an indispensable security blanket in times of her dire need throughout their years together, and she really needed him to pull through for her again.

Kursta owned four thoroughbreds, her most recent acquisition being a black stallion by the name of Bête Noire that she named after Morgan. Morgan was Kursta's pet peeve. She hated that he never showed any interest in her beloved horses. She knew he ignorantly assumed the name referred to the stud's coloring, and she never corrected him. Bête had been on a winning streak and that made Kursta gloat to herself just a little.

Unfortunately, Kursta's other three thoroughbreds weren't performing so well. In fact, they were sucking her dry financially. Freakshot was costing a fortune in training fees. He seemed simply untrainable, not able to complete a single race. She couldn't believe he was sired by a Belmont Stakes champion. Malfeasance had fallen during practice the week before; and GamePlan, a decent runner at one time, was beyond his prime. Fortunately, with Morgan's assistance, she was able to sell fifty percent of GamePlan's ownership interest to his client Hildegard Tanenbaum, which cut some of her losses. With Hilde's recent passing, Kursta wondered who GP's new owner would be.

Kursta previously co-owned another horse with Hilde—a dark bay named Kingston that collapsed and died mysteriously in his stall. Kursta had taken two policies out on him on her own—an all-risk mortality policy with a death benefit, and a policy providing coverage should he become unable to fulfill his potential as a stud.

She became embroiled in a bitter battle with the insurance company when it was discovered the horse's preventive maintenance schedule was not adhered to. Both claims were denied. The insurance adjuster informed Kursta over the phone that according to the veterinary records, the horse received one of the core vaccines three months after the due date.

"But the horse did have the vaccine." Kursta insisted.

"Yes, but not according to the schedule, Ma'am."

"We pay the veterinarian to keep the horses on schedule!" Kursta raised her voice.

"Ma'am, I understand that, but unfortunately, the policies are voided. Maybe your vet will pay you the one hundred fifty thousand dollars."

"*Merde!* You people make it impossible! I don't even understand why we bother to have coverage!" Kursta slammed down the phone and started pacing her office floor.

There was a knock at her door. It opened just wide enough for her assistant's head to poke through.

"Kursta, is everything alright?" The Asian woman, all of four foot eleven with bangs cut perfectly parallel to the bottom of her precise, jet black bob, asked without a smile and blinked hard several times.

"Fine, Anna."

"It's almost five thirty. I need to leave. It's your anniversary, correct?"

"Yes. Thanks for the reminder. I'm right behind you."

"OK, don't forget to lock up. Goodnight and happy anniversary." She blinked again before turning away, leaving the door open.

"Thank you, Anna. Goodnight."

Kursta heard the clicking of Anna's heels followed by

the vibrating of the glass in the front doorframe after she exited. The door needed to be replaced—another item to add to Eddy the Handyman's list.

Kursta gathered her briefcase, purse and blazer, and headed for the lobby. As she stepped on the door threshold, a tall, broad man in his forties with dirty blond, shoulder-length hair stepped into her path, blocking her from going any farther. She gasped.

"Sandy, you scared me." Sandy did odd jobs around the racetrack, but he was no handyman like Eddy.

"I see that." The man looked down at her without a smile.

"What can I help you with?" Kursta focused on maintaining her composure. She knew exactly what he wanted, but he was like an animal with the ability to smell fear. *Stay calm*, she coached herself, wondering if there was anyway she could slip her hand into her purse to grab her LadySmith .38.

He took a step closer so that his black t-shirt under his open canvas jacket brushed her nose. She could smell his perspiration, as her nostrils were at his armpit level. She stepped back. He stepped forward. She backed up a few steps more into her office. He advanced, closing the door behind him.

She was trapped. She knew the chances were slim of getting her hand on her gun before he could rip it away from her. She prepared herself mentally for what might come. She may not make it to Morgan's for dinner. She had seen Eddy wandering around earlier and prayed he would decide to check on her.

"We have business to finish, Kursta."

"I know, Sandy."

"What's the status of the payout?"

"There's no update." She stood, holding her briefcase and blazer in her left hand. Her black leather bag was slung over her right shoulder. Her right hand rested on the zippered opening. She found the slider with her thumb and index finger and tested easing it open without Sandy noticing.

"You still owe me." He closed the gap between them again, forcing Kursta to continue to step backward until the back of her legs pushed up against her desk. He pressed himself against her thighs, staring down her button-up satin violet blouse that was now poofing up to reveal her cleavage. "You owe me fifty thousand dollars, Kursta, and I don't care how you get it. You have two weeks from today."

Kursta recoiled, leaning as far away from him as she could without completely falling on top of the desk. She told herself to be strong, but she couldn't stop herself from trembling uncontrollably.

"I can make your death look like an accident, too." He leaned over her now. "Buzz, buzz." He faked twitching as if he were in convulsions. "Maybe it's a good time for me to take a policy out on you." He smiled widely, revealing a gold crown on a back molar she hadn't noticed before. He took the palm of his hand and pressed down on her chest so that she was all the way down on the desk, flat on her back. A stapler and some papers were sent flying. He pinned himself between her legs, hiking her skirt up in the process, not allowing her to get up. She heard the side seam of her skirt rip. Her chest heaved up and down as her eyes locked with his. Was he going to rape her?

His face was just inches above hers now. She could smell his breath, a putrid combination of whiskey and cigarettes. "Are we clear?" he growled like a predatory cat. He could have his way with her or shred her to pieces.

She nodded quickly, squeezing her eyelids together tightly. She braced herself for what was to come.

He nuzzled his face in her hair and whispered in her ear. "Like I said, two weeks. Don't worry; I'll be giving you reminders. I'll be showing up when you least expect it. Believe me, Kursta, it is in your best interest to pay me as soon as possible. Don't make me remind you too many times. The next one will be much more traumatic than a little tear in your skirt." He paused. "Oh, did I hear it was your anniversary?" She kept her eyes tightly closed and did not respond. "Happy anniversary."

With that, the man suddenly stood up, taking his weight off of her. He turned and walked out of Kursta's office. She waited for the front door to slam. Only then did she open her eyes and get herself to her feet. She pulled her skirt down. She was still trembling. The phone on her desk rang, making her jump. She let it ring two more times before picking up the receiver. Her hands were shaking so bad the receiver slipped out of her fingers as she tried to pick it up and fell over the side of the desk. She picked it up.

"He-Hello?" She could hear the shakiness in her voice.

It was Morgan. "What's wrong?"

"I'm fine. I dropped the phone," she breathed heavily. "I'm just leaving the office now."

Kursta locked up the racing association office, which was on the second floor and overlooked the "backside" of the track—where there were bunks for the groomers and the hot walkers, the paddocks, and the parking lot. She scanned the entire area and scoped out the location of her car before descending the exterior staircase.

"Good night, Kursta," one of the horse groomers called to her from the paddock, startling her a bit.

"Goodnight, Stan," she called back, wondering if Sandy was still in the vicinity.

* * *

Thirty minutes later, Kursta arrived at Morgan's hilltop home. The drive had given her time to compose herself after her run-in with Sandy, but he had injected a fear into her like she had never experienced before in her life. She had no doubt he was capable of carrying out his threat, and the only way to pay him off would be to ask Morgan for the money. She dreaded having this conversation, but she had no choice.

She parked her white Volvo station wagon in Morgan's driveway, and quickly smeared some lipstick over her mouth, looking into the flip-down visor mirror. When she rang the doorbell, Morgan greeted her at the door wearing a red apron over his clothes and a white chef's hat. She could see he was in a playful mood, which was a good sign.

"Chef Boyardee!" Kursta forced a smile and leaned in for an obligatory kiss.

"You like my hat, no?" Morgan mimicked her French accent.

The timer went off in the kitchen and Morgan turned to respond. She started to follow him into the kitchen and he quickly turned around.

"No, no, no!" He shook his finger at her, keeping the French accent. "You stay out of the chef's kitchen." With the kitchen timer still demanding attention, he escorted her to the dining room, where there were two place settings facing each other on one end of the table and a bottle of chardonnay.

"Do have a seat." He pulled a chair out for her so she could sit and then shuffled back into the kitchen. He returned momentarily with a red enamel-covered baking dish.

"You actually made the dinner?" Kursta couldn't believe her eyes when he removed the casserole lid. "Coq au Vin? There's no way."

Morgan smiled, making no admission. He poured them each a glass of the white. "A toast," he said raising his glass, still in his apron and hat. "To happiness and health."

"To happiness and health!" Kursta repeated him. After all, who could argue with that?

Kursta searched for the right time during dinner to broach the subject of a loan with Morgan, but it never materialized. She figured she would have another opportunity as they took their post-dinner conversation to the two Adirondack chairs on the back deck overlooking the lake. A flock of geese had just landed on the water and the sun had barely set, sending streaks of pink and orange across the sky.

"Here." Morgan handed her a card and a small black gift bag with gold tissue before she was completely seated. "Happy anniversary." He leaned over and gave her a small peck on the lips. She couldn't help but hear Sandy's voice saying it in her head.

"What a surprise!" She pulled out the tissue, and tucked inside was a little white leather hinged box. She quickly turned the box over, without Morgan detecting, to see if there was a price tag. She wasn't surprised that he had forgotten to remove it. Five hundred dollars. She only needed $49,500 now.

"Thank you, it's lovely," Kursta pulled the modest diamond pendant necklace out of the box and held each end of the chain up to her neck as a sign for Morgan to clasp it for her.

"It looks nice on you." Morgan poured Kursta another glass of wine. "I'll be right back," he said rather abruptly, and headed back into the house. Kursta wondered what he was doing. She looked out at the water. She remembered when Morgan had taken her out in his canoe—the one and only time. It was about this same time of evening five years ago. It was one of her best memories with Morgan. It had been months since she had been on his back deck. She had forgotten how serene and picturesque it was.

Kursta rehearsed in her head how she would ask for the money. She could just come out and ask for it, but that probably would not go over well after he went out of his way to serve her an authentic French meal and give her a diamond necklace. She, in turn, hadn't even given him a card, but there was still time to give him something he would truly appreciate—a little "cabaret charm." He always liked it when she made the overtures, although it wasn't her favorite thing. In their afterglow, she would ask him for the money.

With the plan in her head, Kursta was ready to execute. She wondered what was keeping Morgan. He had been gone for at least fifteen minutes. She decided to wander back into the house to find him.

She discovered him as he emerged from the bathroom. He was pale and sweaty.

"Is something wrong?" Kursta asked.

"I don't feel well. I just threw up." Morgan was bent over. "Do you feel OK?"

"I'm fine. Do you think it's food poisoning?" Kursta frowned.

Without answering, Morgan made an about-face into the bathroom and closed the door quickly behind him. Kursta knew there would be little chance of having her conversation now. "Do you think it's food poisoning?" Kursta asked again, calling to Morgan from the other side of the door. The noises from the bathroom gave her an affirmative.

After attending to Morgan half the night, bringing him ginger ale and repeatedly emptying out the bowl by his bed—as it became too much of a chore for him to make it to the bathroom—Kursta stared up at the coffered ceiling, wondering how she was going to get herself out of her pickle. Morgan was finally asleep and snoring next to her. She prayed he would be well enough to discuss the subject in the morning.

* * *

The first day's light entered Morgan's bedroom along the edges of the blackout curtains, forming three large neon picture frames in the otherwise dark room. Kursta's sleepless night would soon be over. She lifted her head off the pillow slightly. She thought she detected the faint scent of smoke. Morgan always remarked about her keen sense of smell, comparing her to Weezer; which was really irritating.

Kursta threw the duvet off and slipped out of bed to her feet. She pulled on Morgan's black velour robe lying on the winged back chair by the window, and proceeded down the hall, sniffing the air every few steps to detect where the smoke was coming from. She thought that perhaps Morgan had left the oven on the night before, but the smell was coming from...the study, which she could now see had a light on.

She turned into the room to see the edge of a document on Morgan's desk smoking under the desk lamp. The arm of the lamp had dropped, and the light bulb was touching the paper, causing it to smoke. She quickly lifted the arm of the lamp to discover two incredibly large and beautiful gemstones lying on top of the paper. She tried to move them with her fingers, but they were too hot to touch. One was green and the other a deep sunburst yellow. She quickly lifted up the non-smoking side of the paper to slide the stones onto the desk, and then proceeded to pound the smoking edge with the side of her fist. She saw that the document was the Last Will and Testament of Hildegard Tanenbaum—the co-owner of GamePlan. She wondered if these were Hilde's stones, and was dying to know how Morgan got his hands on them. They certainly dwarfed the diamond in the necklace he gave to her last night!

Morgan stumbled in. "What's going on?"

"I smelled smoke from the bedroom and wandered down the hall to see where it was coming from. A light was left on in your study. When I came in, I saw that the arm of the desk lamp had fallen, and the light bulb almost caught this paper on fire—Hildegard Tanenbaum's will? This is Hildegard's will, so are these her jewels? They must be worth a fortune. What are they—an emerald and a...I don't know, topaz?"

Morgan couldn't believe his eyes. One of the stones had changed colors. He hoped the heat hadn't ruined it. He went to touch it, but it was so hot, he couldn't pick it up. The other stone was equally hot, but still its original color.

"I just replaced the bulb a few days ago. I was out of forty-watt bulbs so replaced it with a hundred-watt instead. Bad idea."

"You could have burned the house down. I'm glad I was able to put it out before it turned into a full-blown fire. You need to be more careful." Kursta paused. "Are you feeling better?"

Morgan rubbed his eyes. "Yes, but dehydrated. You know, I've managed to survive in this house all these years without a catastrophe. You don't need to scold me like a child."

"I wasn't scolding you. Did these stones belong to Hildegard?"

"You're just like Weezer when he was chasing rabbits—relentless."

Another Weezer reference! Kursta knew Morgan was right, but she couldn't help herself from continuing her line of questioning. "So, whom do they belong to now, now that Hilde is dead? Did she leave them to you?"

"No, they don't belong to me. You know I can't talk about my clients. It's confidential."

"Does the attorney-client privilege apply to dead people?" she pressed.

"There's an heir."

"So, who is GP's new owner?"

"Hilde's niece. You'll meet her when I bring her out to the track to see the horse." He shut off the lamp and put his hand on the small of Kursta's back, coaxing her out of the room.

As they turned down the hall toward the kitchen, Kursta asked, "They're worth hundreds of thousands of dollars at least, don't you think?"

"Probably. It doesn't matter. You want some coffee?"

Kursta fell momentarily silent as she watched Morgan proceed to put a filter into his old coffee pot.

"Do you still have that French Press I bought you for Christmas?" She hinted at wanting better coffee.

Morgan sighed and bent down to get it out of the cabinet. "I'm not sure all the parts are there. Do you mind helping?"

Kursta took over the set-up of the coffee press while Morgan put the teakettle on the stove to boil water.

"So, are you in trouble again?" Morgan asked bluntly. "You're awfully interested in those jewels. Do you need some money?"

Kursta knew Morgan didn't mean the question as an offer, and that he was upset with her. She had been waiting to have this conversation, but she knew it wasn't going to be pleasant. She started crying.

"Here we go." Morgan sighed. "Tell me what's going on." His voice was low.

Kursta took a deep breath. "I got some bad news on the insurance claims for Kingston."

"What do you mean, bad news?"

"The insurance company said they won't pay since the vaccine schedule was not adhered to. He had one of his shots three months too late."

"Is that stipulated in the policies?"

"Yes."

"Do they think the delayed shot was responsible for his death? I thought he collapsed, like a heart attack."

"They haven't determined the cause of death yet, but it really doesn't matter. Since the preventive schedule was not followed they will not pay on either policy. Now, I'm out one hundred fifty thousand dollars."

"You're out that money? I know that's how much the policies were worth, but are you really in that much debt? Was Kingston worth that much?"

Kursta swallowed hard. Her neck was tight. "Let's just say I was really counting on that money."

The teakettle whistled. Morgan turned the burner off and poured the water over the coffee that Kursta had placed in the French press carafe.

"I can't give you that kind of money," Morgan locked eye contact with her.

Tears welled up in Kursta's eyes. "All I really need is fifty thousand right now."

"For what? Are you fifty thousand dollars in debt?"

Kursta started sobbing.

"What could you have possibly purchased that cost that much money?" He was clearly angry. Kursta had never seen that expression on his face before. His face was so red she thought his head might spout off. "Why do you assume that I'll always bail you out, Kursta? That I'll always pick up the pieces? Don't you understand that your behavior around money is a big reason why I don't want to be in this relationship anymore?"

He wasn't saying anything she didn't already know; it was just hard to hear it. She stood looking at him for a moment before heading down the hallway to put her clothes on and leave.

Chapter 7

When Morgan heard Kursta slam the front door on her way out, he decided the first thing he was going to do was make a fresh pot of his usual drip brew. He didn't need no stinkin' pretentious French coffee. While it was brewing, he returned to his study to take another look at the stones. He switched on the lamp again, which was now cool, and both stones were green and identical again! The will was only slightly singed on one edge. He was relieved that there was no apparent damage to the stones. He wondered if the new owner of Clobert's—the famous master jeweler, Julian Kleptstein, whom he had never seen but had heard so much about from the radio ads—would be clever enough to discover the secret about one of them.

Morgan had read articles in the local paper that said the plans for Clobert's new design institute and gemology research center would end up taking nearly an entire city block in the middle of town. The original building, which had been the first savings and loan in the county, was undergoing extensive renovation. The entrance was surrounded by scaffolding, plywood, and blue tarps. A makeshift sign read, "Open During Construction."

When Morgan entered the jewelry showroom, he immediately recognized one of the men standing behind the counter. It was the man at Hildegard's rosary that was stroking Ruby's hair. The one he had warned her about when he dropped her off in the church parking lot.

Perhaps he was just a clerk there.

The man recognized Morgan, too, and went right up to him. "Hey, how are you? What can I help you with today?"

Morgan smiled. "Oh, yeah. Hey, how are you? I'm looking for the owner."

"You're looking at him," the man put his arms up and smiled.

"You're Julian Kleptstein? The guy in all the radio ads? You own Clobert's?"

Kleptstein nodded. "Is it so hard to believe?" he asked.

"Well, your voice just sounds different on the radio."

"What can I help you with today?" Kleptstein looked at Morgan's briefcase. "Did you bring something in you'd like to show me?"

Against Morgan's better judgment he nodded his head.

"Please excuse the mess, and the noise. Let's go back to my office." Julian Kleptstein directed Morgan to a room at the back of the showroom. "My best loop is in here." He closed the door behind them. "Plus, it's less noisy." He asked, "How's Ruby?"

"Yes, thank you for asking and for helping us with Ruby the other day. She's been through a lot." Morgan was anxious to get to the matter at hand since he didn't do the smart thing and walk out when he could have.

"Sit down, please." Kleptstein motioned to a burgundy leather chair next to a desk where he sat on the other side. A microscope stood stoutly on one corner. Kleptstein pulled a loop from the top drawer of the desk. Morgan snapped open his briefcase and revealed the two velvet pouches, one blue, the other black. He handed them to Kleptstein, who gently drew the first tear-dropped stone from its blue cocoon.

"This is a very large stone—thirty karats, perhaps," he concluded matter-of-factly. "Let's take a look at the other one." He pulled the stone from its soft black womb.

"Twins?" Kleptstein asked quizzically. "Tell me what you know about these gems. Do you know their history?"

Morgan swallowed. "There is a GIA grade study on the one in the black pouch that was done in 1973." He handed Kleptstein the paperwork. "However, there is no paperwork on the one you're holding."

Kleptstein put the loop to his right eye and held the stone from the blue pouch up to the loop. He rotated it in his fingers and squinted. He turned his gaze to Morgan. "There is no stamp on this one. Is that all you know about it?"

Morgan sensed Kleptstein thought he was hiding something. "Yep. That's why I brought them here to you. You're the expert." Morgan's voice was a bit sing-song.

"I'll run some tests as well as a search on the GIA laser stamp and be back in touch." Kleptstein stood, and Morgan followed. "You'll have to sign some paperwork before you leave. Does anyone know you have these stones in your possession?"

Chapter 8

Kleptstein's fascination with Ruby ignited into a fierce obsession. He kept replaying her rosary fainting spell in his head. She was a fine-boned baby bird that had dropped out of its nest and serendipitously into his hands. He closed his eyes and tried to remember her scent, the slight weight of her body against him, the soft feathers of her dark hair on his forearms.

He saw Ruby's face everywhere he went—on billboards, in windows, in mirrors, even in the glass of the showroom jewelry cases. Every woman's face he encountered was Ruby's at first, until coming into focus, revealing her less than satisfactory features. Kleptstein was seized with a desperate, debilitating desire. As each day of his existence slithered into the next, it became obvious that he couldn't be just any man to Ruby.

The nights he spent hanging on to her every note at Curiocity barely carried him through his never-ending days at the gemology institute. He had made it a habit to give her a dozen ruby red roses each night after the show, but he wasn't sure she appreciated them any more. Occasionally, he would chat with her after a set, but he always did most of the talking. He sensed trepidation in her. He wished he could make it go away, but he didn't know how. He feared the "someday drink" she agreed to would never be poured.

As the days grew into weeks, so did Kleptstein's angst that Ruby would never truly understand the depth of his feelings for her. He became determined to overcome his insufficiency in self-confidence and his overabundance in self-loathing. He committed himself to breaking his silence. If he didn't follow through, it might kill him.

The fateful night fell on a Friday. Kleptstein found his familiar barstool in the front row on the right-hand side of the stage. Chai, the Curiocity M.C., got up to the mic, told a few off-colored jokes, as usual, and with a wild smile announced, "We are pleased to introduce a new act to Curiocity."

Kleptstein froze in the middle of his sloe gin fizz. The audience cheered and whistled more fervently than Kleptstein could ever remember. The red roses he'd brought for Ruby dropped out of his hand to the floor.

As soon as Chai stepped off the stage in his baby blue crushed velvet sports coat, Kleptstein stood up and grabbed him by the arm.

"Hey, Chai, what happened to Ruby?"

Chai looked over at Kleptstein's hand on his coat, wriggled out from Kleptstein's grip and brushed off his sleeve.

"She quit. It's all right, though, Man. That swanky blues, it's just not what people dig anymore. Now, this band, Industrial Sturgeon, they're real. Their songs cut to the core of the fundamental human dilemma—primal desire versus civil imposition." Chai spoke with a severe conviction. "All Ruby could sing about was, 'I lost my baby.' They're saying, 'I lost my instinct.' Boom."

"But, Ruby could sing. I can't believe this." Kleptstein was amped like he could run a mile. "Well, Vin's really made a mistake this time. Is she singing anywhere else?" Kleptstein grew breathless and warm. He dug a finger in between his neck and collar to give him some breathing room. His forehead beaded in a cool sweat.

"Man, are you okay?" Chai looked at him with wide eyes and raised eyebrows.

Kleptstein realized his panic was surfacing. He tried

to hold back the ocean of nausea flooding his gut. "Yeah, yeah, it's just hot in here. I got a business proposition for Ruby. It's something she's got to jump on right away, you know? I need to find her. See, I've got this friend who..." In his moments of despair, Kleptstein was quick at making up cockamamie stories.

"Listen, I don't think Ruby's going to be doing any more singing." Chai got close to Klept's ear. "Rumor has it, she's a rich fool and inherited a hefty chunk from some dead relative she hadn't seen in years. Man, why can't I have relatives like that? Mine are always asking me for money."

The band started up. It was impossible to hear over the screech and fusion of sounds slamming together like sequential car crashes.

"Aren't they great?" Chai nodded his head to the sounds and smiled. "Listen, I'm not supposed to give out personal information on our gigs." Chai passed his hand over his gelled hair and pulled a cigarette out of thin air. "But, if you go up to the bar and you're real nice to Suki, she just might give you Ruby's number. OK, Pal?"

Kleptstein could tell he was wasting his time with Chai.

"Are you sure you're okay?" Chai looked genuinely concerned. "You're white as a specter. Here," Chai handed him a complimentary drink ticket. "Go get yourself a stiff one."

Suki Giles obviously could see right through Kleptstein."I know you ain't got a friend who's an agent or a scout, unless he's a boy scout." Suki laughed in short sequential bursts like she was having a seizure. She paused to take a puff of her Swisher Sweet and scribbled a number on a bar napkin. "Call her, but don't you dare tell her Suki gave you the number. Good luck trying to catch her. I've barely spoken to her in the last two weeks and I live with her." She handed the napkin to him.

Kleptstein looked down at the unusually neat handwriting and back up at Suki. "Chai tells me Ruby's rolling in the dough. Is that why she quit? Vinnie didn't can her, did he?" Kleptstein was fishing, but surprisingly, Suki didn't bite. Instead, she patted his hand patronizingly.

"Must be nice. All I could ever do is dream about that happening to me." The truth was that Kleptstein had plenty of money, but that wouldn't help his case. He sensed it was futile trying to pump Suki any longer. He had Ruby's number. He would find out himself.

"Can I get you a drink?" Suki changed the subject.

"Nah, thanks. You're a doll." He held up the napkin and smiled faintly. He folded it up and slid it into his shirt pocket.

After getting a busy signal seven times, the operator confirmed for fifty cents that Ruby's line was off the hook. Kleptstein drove by her house and saw a light shine through the lace curtains. He wanted to go up and knock on her door, but then he would have to explain how he knew where she lived. This was going too far. What was he thinking? He would have to schedule an appointment with Margie Fox soon and adjust his meds. He decided to head home but not until he had circled Ruby's house one last time first.

At home, Kleptstein leaned back in his recliner, trying to get his mind off Ruby. He wanted to call her again, but it was too late. After resolving himself to the fact that he wouldn't speak to her that night, he finally fell asleep in the middle of a re-run of his favorite Night Gallery episode, "Talking Tina," with his orange cat curled up at his feet.

Chapter 9

While Kursta suffered from interminable financial failure, she was quite successful at riding the crest of the racing social circle. Her latest obsession was orchestrating a slew of clandestine parties, fondly called the "Bashes," sponsored by the local racehorse owners association. She was placed in charge of these galas for her talent in outdoing herself every time. Each party proved to be more tantalizingly bizarre than the previous. Kursta was a firm believer in the power of fantasy, and organizing the Bashes temporarily relieved her of her chronic ennui.

These parties were not for everyone. They certainly were not for Morgan. Kursta recalled that he had attended a couple of the Bashes, but she decided to leave him at home after he accused them of "providing an opportunity for deviant individuals to prey on the vulnerabilities of the innocent." He questioned her about rumors that people were sometimes pick-pocketed, and one woman had even suffered a seizure after drinking the "Evening Initiator"—a drink served to guests as they were greeted at the door. Morgan half jested that horse tranquilizers were dropped into the drinks of the guests.

It was the middle of the month, and that meant it was time to print the invitations for the next Bash. Kursta decided to try a new printer, one closer to the racing association office and supposedly cheaper.

She opened the glass door and the bells hanging from the inside handle announced her arrival. A robust man with jet-black hair stood in an open area of the store, surrounded by copiers. He displayed a hearty smile that seemed to say, "How may I help you?"

She immediately concluded that he wasn't from the city. No one smiled a full smile in the city. You were lucky to get two tightly stretched lips curved over a façade of tolerance.

She pulled the design out of her briefcase and began to explain what she wanted to the man, who kept smiling. It suddenly dawned on her that he didn't work there.

"I'm sorry." She returned a smile in her embarrassment.

"No problem." His smile showed no sign of fading. "I'm looking for the clerk myself. I like your accent. Is it French?"

Out of nowhere, a frantic young man with tattered clothing, a beard that could have doubled as a bird's nest, and bare feet burst through the shop doors. He pushed Kursta out of his way and rushed the front counter.

"Who works here?!" He rasped out of breath.

"I beg your pardon!" Kursta was insulted.

"Is something wrong? Can I help you?" the once-smiling man asked.

The young man, disoriented with his eyes ablaze, turned sharply and grabbed Kursta by the collar of her blouse. He swung her around so that her back was against his chest and his forearm pressed against her throat while he held a knife just under her jaw. Once again, she found herself in a situation where she could not get to her loaded S&W Ladysmith in time.

"Just take it easy, Guy." The smiling man spoke calmly and made slow, small steps toward the man, who resembled a trapped animal.

"You want to help me? Get someone who works here!" His voice had an odd, muffled quality.

From the back room, a blond teenager with a bad case of acne moseyed in, drinking a jumbo soda and wearing a blue vest. "I was on my break. Sorry, I'm the only one here." He spoke before he had assessed the situation.

The kid's entrance gave the smiling man just enough time to grab the crazed man's wrist brandishing the knife. He shielded Kursta's throat with a protective hand, but his fingers were sliced in the process. Kursta elbowed her assailant in the gut, wriggled down to the floor, and got away to a comfortable distance.

Instead of going back for Kursta, the scruffy young man wasted no time making his way back to the counter. He held up the blood-streaked knife.

"You know I'll use it. Empty the register now!" he screamed at the kid.

The cut man charged toward the animal from behind at a diagonal and grabbed the back of his dusty denim jacket. He jerked him back with great force, killing his balance, and then shoved him face-first into the wall adjacent to the counter. The knife dropped to the floor. The cut man kicked it out of reach. It spun around as it slid in Kursta's direction, coming to rest only a few inches from her foot. The cut man kept his grip on the wild guy as he slid to the floor, face down.

"Call 9-1-1," the cut man instructed Kursta. The kid was nowhere in sight. The young man started writhing under his grasp. "First, look for something I can tie this guy's hands with. Is there a binder tie or a rope?"

Kursta scanned the area behind the counter. She spotted a couple of bungee cords used to hang banners. She went around the counter, grabbed them, and brought them to Kleptstein. Her heart was pounding.

The young man was thrashing about. The cut man managed to pulled the guy's wrists as closely together as he could, and Kursta wound one of the cord's around them until the cut man could take over. He tied the bungee cord in a strange knot she hadn't seen before. She saw that his hand was bleeding a lot. She handed him the other cord, which he barely managed to tie around the guy's ankles without being kicked in the face. Kursta called 9-1-1.

"Okay, Man, you win. I'm not going to fight you anymore. Can't you just let me go?"

"You're not going anywhere until the cops take you away." The man directed his attention to Kursta. "Are you okay?" he asked her.

She nodded in complete amazement.

The cops arrived sooner than expected. Perhaps the clerk had called them from a phone in the backroom. The officers asked Kursta and the cut man for statements and indicated they would be in touch for any further action. They recommended the man have his hand checked out.

"I didn't catch your name," the cut man asked Kursta. "I'm Julian. Julian Kleptstein."

"Kursta Blithey. I've heard your radio ads. You own Clobert's, right?"

He nodded.

"And you tackle bad guys in your spare time?" She winked, flirtatiously. She couldn't believe what she had just witnessed. She was standing in the presence of a hero. They both could have been killed. This man's quick action seemed to come so naturally. Kursta couldn't help but notice that this man had something Morgan had never possessed—a natural sense of self and spontaneity. "I've got to ask you, do you know martial arts or...?"

"Oh, a little bit. I was in the army for four years right after high school, before I came back to help my parents with the business. You learn things. It was no big deal."

But it was a big deal, Kursta thought to herself. "I wonder what's going to happen to him."

"Honestly, they'll probably hold him for a day or two and let him go. Our county jail is so full of criminals."

Kursta knew his words to be true. She gazed into eyes. Where had he been hiding himself? She couldn't believe that she had never met him in all the years that she had lived in Tolstoy. She had even been in the jewelry store a few times. She told him she remembered his parents.

"Yeah, my dad is at Meadowview Convalescent now. It's so sad, he doesn't even know who I am. I go to see him just about every week. I tell him about the design institute, you know. I say, 'Hey Dad, your dream is coming true. I'm doing it for you, Dad.' But he doesn't comprehend."

Adrenaline was still pumping through Kursta. "I can't thank you enough for what you did. People just don't put themselves on the line like that for other people. Except military people, I guess." She felt curiously vulnerable in that moment, something she hadn't felt in a long time. "Let me buy you dinner," Kursta blurted out before she realized what she had said. "I meant to say, take you to the urgent care. But, I would like to take you to dinner, too." She felt her face turn red.

"Really, it's not necessary." Julian looked down at his hand. He had grabbed a wad paper towels and was squeezing it to the stop the bleeding, but it was soaked through.

"You need medical attention. There's an urgent care around the corner. I will take you. I insist."

Kursta was more than thrilled to take Julian Kleptstein to the urgent care. Thirty-five stitches later, she insisted on taking him to dinner at Chez Jeanty, just a few blocks from Clobert's.

"The bone marrow is to die for!" Kursta oozed with giddy schoolgirl excitement as they settled into a banquette and opened their menus. It wasn't long before they began reliving the sequence of their harrowing event, laughing and congratulating each other.

"This calls for some bubbly!" Kursta announced and summoned their waiter over for a bottle of Veuve Cliquot.

A young blond woman seated alone on the cushion side of the table next to them intruded on their conversation. "I'm sorry to interrupt," she spoke as if she were on fast forward, "but are you the couple that just apprehended the man at Premier Printing a few hours ago? It's been all over the radio."

The thin bubble insulating Kursta with this special man had just been popped. Her surroundings immediately expanded from their intimate space to the expanse of the room. She looked around. Just who had heard them? Was she talking loudly? Her eyes settled on the young woman next to her.

Kleptstein spoke one word: "Yeah."

The woman looked down at the bandage on his hand. "You were cut. Did you have stitches?"

Kleptstein put a finger between his collar and his neck. "Yeah, but I'm alright."

A young man came up and sat down opposite of the young woman.

"Honey," the young woman beamed, "this is the couple that took that guy down at Premier Printing."

"We are not a couple," Kleptstein corrected her. He smiled in Kursta's direction politely. "We were just celebrating our escape." He laughed. "Would you like to join us for a toast?" Kleptstein looked over at Kursta. He didn't notice her disappointment. He asked the waiter for two more glasses.

The young man gave the toast. "To two of Tolstoy's hometown heroes! We need more people like you in our community." A few people at surrounding tables had heard them.

"Here, here," an older man's voice said from the table behind him. When Kursta turned to see where the voice came from, she saw an older couple raise their glasses and smile.

"Congratulations!" a woman said from another table.

"Cheers to our hometown heroes!" Another man in the corner raised his glass.

When it was time for their check, the waiter informed them that their tab had already been taken care of. "The Cliquot was almost a hundred dollars itself," Kursta remarked as they exited the restaurant.

"Where should I drop you off? Your house?" Kursta asked Kleptstein as they climbed into her Volvo. It was almost dark.

"I walked down to the print shop from the jewelry store. You can drop me off there."

"Well, thank you for an exciting afternoon and a

wonderful evening." Kursta smiled brightly in the darkness of her car.

"What are you going to do about your invitations?" he asked her.

"I'll take them back to Premier in the morning. I need to get them out tomorrow." A thought occurred to Kursta. "Would you like to accompany me to the Bash?"

Chapter 10

Morgan received a call from a woman with a Spanish accent at Clobert's informing him that Mr. Kleptstein was ready to meet with him about the diamonds. Morgan wanted her to clarify whether they were ready to be picked up, but the woman's repeated response was that Mr. Kleptstein wanted to meet with him first. As Morgan got into his car, he kicked himself again for not going to another jeweler.

The story about Kleptstein and Kursta apprehending the homeless drug addict was splashed all over the media. There was even a banner hanging above Premier Printers reading, "Thank you, Hometown Heroes!" Morgan disdained the multiplying threads attaching him to this odd duck that seemed to change with his surroundings and the people he associated with. Morgan couldn't shake the memory of how Kleptstein looked at Ruby that day at the church, how he caressed her head and arms as she was passed out on the pew. Kleptstein reminded him of someone who would drug pretty girls and take advantage of them. And now he was being called a hero along with Kursta Blithey? As Kursta would say, *Mon Dieu!*

Morgan parked the car on the street in front of the jewelry store and entered the building through its still less-than-obvious entrance.

"Mr. Morgan." Kleptstein offered his un-bandaged hand in an awkward left-handed shake.

Morgan reciprocated with a deliberate tight squeeze.

"You're quite the hero."

"Well, it was a team effort. Former councilwoman Kursta Blithey was a big help. She really held her own. I couldn't have apprehended the bum without her."

Morgan nodded. "Obviously, you are not someone to be messed with. You're a badass. I saw the video clip on the news. Where'd you get your moves, huh?" Morgan squeezed Kleptstein's bicep with one arm while patting him firmly on the back with the other. Both men laughed, thinly veiling their sizing-up of one another.

"Come on back to my office," Kleptstein motioned with a half-smile. "Have a seat." The pouches were on the desk. Kleptstein moved around to the other side of the desk and got down to business. "These jewels are fancy green diamonds, extremely rare. As you noted, one has a GIA grade study. We know a bit about that one. It's actually quite famous and comes from a mine in Central Africa. It was discovered in 1943 and is known as the Finian Star. Finian is an Irish name, as you probably know. One of the former owners was likely Irish, although not all the owners were registered."

"What's the reference to Star?" Morgan asked.

"While I'm not exactly sure, it's not a reference to the shape of the diamond. Many famous diamonds have the word 'star' in their names. And of course, there are many popular and historical correlations between stars and diamonds." Kleptstein paused for a moment and picked up the black pouch. He coaxed the stone from its cocoon.

He continued, "Green diamonds are so interesting because their color comes from radiation deep in the earth. They are much more brilliant than emeralds. It is rare to see such consistent color throughout the stone, like we see in this one. This is the one with the GIA grade. It is registered in the name of Hildegard Tanenbaum, whom I assume was your client." He looked up at Morgan, who didn't respond. Kleptstein continued, "Prior to her ownership, it was owned by an anthropologist from

India, a Nuhr Dhanuka. I'm not sure how Ms. Tanenbaum acquired it from him. Do you know?"

Morgan ignored the question. "How much is it worth?" he asked.

"Based on our analysis of the stone, along with research on comparable gems, for which there are only a few in the world, we estimate the value at 1.2 million dollars, U.S."

Morgan's eyes widened for a moment. Expressionless, Kleptstein made eye contact, waiting for Morgan to say something. Morgan remained silent, so Kleptstein continued.

"Now, let's talk about the other stone." He pulled it out of its blue pouch. "As we established, it has no GIA grade, but I would recommend it."

"I'm paying you to grade it." Morgan shifted in his seat.

"Yes, of course. However, it is always good to have a formal GIA grade study done. It helps establish the value and registers the stone. We can take care of that for you."

"You can tell me the value, though, right?"

"An approximate value. Again, the GIA study would give it a more definitive valuation. Is there some reason you do not want to do the GIA study? I would send it off myself and ensure it was tracked appropriately." He waited for Morgan to answer.

"Tell me how much you think it's worth," Morgan insisted.

"Although these two diamonds look identical to the untrained eye, they are actually quite different from each other. This ungraded stone is of superior quality. For one, it is slightly larger, although hard to tell; and the clarity is better. It is a VVS1 as opposed to the VS1 of the other diamond." He set the two stones side by side.

Morgan waited for Kleptstein to mention the stone's color-changing ability.

"The value of this stone," Kleptstein pointed to the unregistered one, "is estimated at seven million dollars.

It closely resembles a conflict diamond originating in the same time period as the other. I would need more time in order to make a positive identification. Again, the GIA study would do that."

"A conflict diamond? What does that even mean?"

Kleptstein leaned forward across the desk, closing the gap between them to a matter of inches, while sliding his bandaged hand over the stones. He came close enough for Morgan to catch a whiff of his aftershave.

"Are you really so naive? Where did you get this diamond? Did it belong to Ms. Tanenbaum as well?" Kleptstein locked eyes with Morgan.

"I don't see how that is any of your business." Morgan swallowed.

"You need to tell your new client that precautions are necessary when owning stones of this caliber. These are no ordinary diamonds, and I will be tracking them, Mr. Morgan. I have an obligation to my field, to my profession as a gemologist."

Morgan wrapped his hand around Kleptstein's bandaged wrist and began to squeeze. "Give me the diamonds."

Kleptstein clutched the jewels as tightly as he could in his wounded hand, but he knew he would not be able to hang on for long. The pain was excruciating. "Please allow me to send the ungraded one out for a GIA study. We can learn more about it together. It could end up being worth more than my estimate."

Morgan noticed the shift in Kleptstein's tone. "Thank you, but I'll be taking my business elsewhere." His grip tightened around Kleptstein's wrist.

Kleptstein clenched his jaw in response to the pain. "I have connections to every jeweler in the world, Mr. Morgan. We are a small network."

"What is your point?" Morgan kept calm.

"I can't let you take the diamonds." Kleptstein's agitation bloomed.

"Watch me." Morgan's tone was confident. "I know

about you."

"What do you know about me?" Kleptstein was getting hot under the collar and pried a finger from his left hand between it and his neck.

"When was the last time you saw Margie Fox?"

Chapter 11

Ruby woke up an hour early that Sunday despite enduring a nearly sleepless night. Morgan was to pick her up at 10 a.m. sharp to introduce her to GamePlan, her new racehorse, and then take her to the Green Gable Estate, Hilde's last residence before being admitted to Meadowview. She made sure she was ready to go in plenty of time.

She clicked on the television. It was the local morning news. They were interviewing Julian Kleptstein.

Suki stumbled in from the other room wearing her kitty pj's. "Hey, it's the creepy guy that gives you roses after every show." She reached for her cat-eyed glasses that were left on the end table and flopped herself on the couch.

Ruby admitted she was oddly interested in Kleptstein's recent hero status.

"It's hard to believe the creepy rose guy could apprehend a dangerous criminal, don't you think? Maybe there's more to him than meets the eye," Suki added as she pulled a Sherpa throw over her legs.

Ruby nodded, half-listening. She pulled the ottoman close to the TV and sat down to get a better view of the screen.

The young female reporter asked Kleptstein what possessed him to confront the aggressor.

"He had the woman in his grasp," Kleptstein answered, breathing hard as if he were back at the scene. "He was holding a knife to her throat. I couldn't just stand there and do nothing." The news cut to a hazy black-and-white video of the clerk walking in and paused it.

"That's the moment you acted," the reporter stated, but it was more of a question.

"That's right," Kleptstein jumped in. "The store clerk walking into the room distracted the guy, giving me a chance to pry the knife away from him."

"Injuring you in the process. Is it true you had thirty-five stitches as a result of the incident?"

"At least." Kleptstein held up his arm to the camera for a tight close-up on his bandaged hand.

"And the woman's life you saved. Who was that?"

"She was another customer there at the print shop." The shot then cut to a professional headshot of the woman.

"She's not just any woman. That's Kursta Blithey, former city councilwoman and Manager of Diamond Head Stables, which has been the subject of a recent state investigation." The reporter turned to Kleptstein and held the microphone out to him.

"I don't know anything about that," he looked at the camera.

The reporter turned her gaze to the camera. "And there you have it. Julian Kleptstein, world renown gemologist and Tolstoy's local, hometown hero." Suddenly the woman was overcome by a fleeting Spanish accent. "Alejandra Castillo Ariano." She nodded. "Back to you."

"You know what's so weird?" Ruby said. "I had a bunch of hang up calls on the answering machine the other night."

Suki got a weird look on her face.

"Why are you looking like that?" Ruby asked.

"I'm sorry, Tuesday." Tuesday was Suki's pet name for Ruby, as in Ruby Tuesday.

"What? What are you sorry for?" Ruby heard a car outside. She could see it was Morgan's Mercedes through the sheer curtains.

"I gotta go. What do you have to tell me?"

"Your lawyer's here?"

"Yeah."

"I gave the creepy rose guy your number."

"You did?" Ruby was confused. "Why would you do that?"

"I don't know. It was poor judgment on my part. He seemed desperate to find you and I heard he might have a job for you."

"A job? I'm not looking for a job right now." Ruby and Suki had worked their whole lives since high school. Even while Ruby was going to college, she had to work part time.

Ruby was careful not to mention the racehorse, the estate, or any of the money to Suki—yet. It was too soon. She didn't even tell her she had a half-brother. All Suki knew was Ruby was meeting her attorney that day to hopefully find out what she had inherited.

"Again, I'm very sorry, Tuesday." Suki puckered her lip the way she always did when she felt guilty.

"It's OK." Ruby walked over to her and gave her a hug goodbye. "He's harmless... maybe."

Ruby looked out the window. "He's getting out of his car. I gotta go." She blew Suki a kiss and left through the front door just as Morgan was making his way up the sidewalk.

"So, this is the house you're having landlord troubles over?" Ruby could tell Morgan was not impressed. Admittedly, it did need a new roof and a paint job.

"Yeah." Ruby was distracted by Suki, who was gawking out the window at them, waving. "That's my roommate."

Morgan waved to the cat-spectacled woman inside with the pink and purple hair. They turned back toward Morgan's car. He opened the passenger door for Ruby.

"Like I said, I'll be happy to help with your landlord issues, but honestly, Ms. Sans, you don't need to live in this house anymore."

Ruby shot him a look. "What's wrong with my house?"

"Sorry, I didn't mean anything by it. Wait until you see your new house."

Your new house, Ruby said to herself. "This is all so much to take in." Ruby inhaled deeply.

"Well, let's focus on one thing at a time today; first of which is getting acquainted with your new horse GamePlan." Morgan closed her door and got in on his side.

Ruby wanted to bring up the topic of Hilde owning two racehorses so late in her life with Morgan, but wasn't convinced she'd get the straight scoop. She wondered if he had really coerced or at least persuaded Hilde to invest in GamePlan. Ruby could hardly contain the nervous energy inside her as they exited the freeway. She had seen the track from a distance many times and had always wondered what it would be like to see a horse race.

Morgan led her to the paddock area. There were long rows of stables, which reminded Ruby of her summer visits to the county fair with Hilde. Seeing the show horses was her favorite stop on the long walk from the entry gate to the midway rides.

A few horses stuck their heads out over their gates. Others could be heard snorting as they ate. Morgan and Ruby made their way behind the stables toward the track.

"There's GP's manager and trainer," Morgan said as he pointed toward a man a distance away watching the track.

Owen Kierney was a dark redhead about six foot three. His skin was an intriguing bronze with an undertone of freckles on his forearms and the bridge of his pointy nose.

"So this is GamePlan's new co-owner, is it Mil?" Owen reached his hand out to Ruby and gave hers a firm, confident, lingering squeeze. "Sorry to hear about your aunt, Ms. Sans. She was a great lady and we all loved her dearly. And boy, did she love her GP." Owen looked into the distance. Ruby and Morgan looked in the same direction to see a dark bay horse rounding the far side of the track toward them. Ruby loved watching the motion of the horse's muscles under the satin skin, a powerful machine. The pounding of his hooves grew louder as he approached.

Regardless of the circumstances around her ownership, she got caught up in the moment. "He's beautiful!" Ruby squealed as the horse and rider flew past them.

Owen held a stopwatch in his hand. "That was a good lap," Owen chuckled in delight, showing a row of perfectly white teeth. "He's been running hot. The upcoming race should be good." He locked eyes with Ruby for a moment, giving her a jolt.

After making a cool-down lap, the jockey brought the horse to the stable area.

"He's so big." Ruby stared up at the horse with the jockey still in the saddle.

"He's sixteen hands," the jockey said in a nasally tone. Ruby reached up to touch the horse but stopped short.

"It's OK," the jockey nodded.

Owen told Ruby that GamePlan or "GP" had come from a strong, noble line of racers known for a discriminating mark of white where Mother Nature had kissed their foreheads. He'd been given a big smooch of a star on his forehead and a snip between his nostrils. Ruby was instantly smitten with him.

Roman Drewster had been GamePlan's jockey for quite some time. He professed that he knew the horse instinctively, and that the two made a compatible pair. Roman joked that he was more fond of horses than people.

"And that works out well because few people are fond of Mr. Drewster," Owen jibed.

Roman chimed in, "I must admit, my temperament is identical to my stature: short."

"Here are a few more fun facts, shall we say, about Roman Drewster, Ms. Sans," Owen had just a twang of an accent that Ruby could not pick out. "I swear, this guy," Owen pointed up to Roman, "must have been a racehorse in his former life because he cannot stand still to save his life. And his respiratory system exudes Marlboro filters. And his liver is pickled in Blue Sapphire. But…" Ruby sensed Owen was going to say something more serious. "When it comes to racing, I reverently proclaim that there are few jockeys in the world that rival Roman Leroy Drewster."

Roman shook his head and smirked. "You know my middle name is not Leroy." They all laughed.

Ruby informed Owen Kierney that she was interested in getting to know GamePlan as a racer. She knew little about his history and thought after speaking with Owen that she might be able to better tell whether or not it would be a wise investment to keep her share of the horse.

Although Ruby directed her conversation to Owen Kierney, Roman couldn't help but jump in. "GP has an excellent team looking after him. And being that your aunt has made sure that he's been taken care of in her absence, I don't see any reason why the situation should change. This animal is basically taking care of himself."

"And you, too, Mr. Drewster." Ruby responded.

"Yes, Ms. Sans, I would be lying if I said GP wasn't good to me. But, he was good to your aunt, too. See, the problem is, you just don't know enough about the sport. And that's not your fault. You've just entered a whole new world." He made a gesture as though he was holding a globe in his hands and that it just exploded. Poof! "I strongly suggest you come to a race. You've never been to a race before, have you Ms. Sans?" Roman continued.

"No, no I haven't." Ruby felt out of her element. She wondered if her aunt had felt that way, too.

Roman kept talking while Owen just stood and smiled at the two in silence, revealing two deep dimples in his cheeks, his tan arms crossed in front of him. Ruby noticed Morgan had wandered off.

"Well, you're in for quite a treat," Roman continued. "I've been around the track since I was thirteen. Trust me, you're in for something good. Why, Owen and I'll even introduce you to some other horse owners and jockeys."

"I'd really like that." Ruby noticed Morgan walking back towards them from one of the buildings.

"If we win, Ms. Sans. If we win."

Ruby reached up again and ran her hand down the horse's sleek neck.

Roman droned on, "What you do with your horse is clearly up to you, Ms. Sans, in conjunction with the other owner, of course. I've heard there are a few people chomping at the bit to snatch up GP. If you and the other owner wanted to sell him, there's no doubt, he would get you a pretty penny. But, the situation as it stands has been working out good for the horse."

"Who is the other owner?" Ruby asked.

From a distance behind her, Ruby heard a woman's voice calling out. Roman and Owen turned to see a strawberry-blond, middle-aged woman almost running their way, carrying an attaché case.

"Well, speak of the devil." Owen smiled, showing off his dimples again.

"Kursta Blithey, General Manager of Diamond Head Stables," the woman held her hand out to Ruby, a bit breathless. "You must be Hildegard's niece. I am sorry to hear about your aunt."

Suddenly it dawned on Ruby that this was the Kursta Blithey that had been on the news with Kleptstein. "Hey, you're a celebrity! I saw you on the news today!"

"You could say I was just in the wrong place at the right time," Kursta laughed it off.

"I've heard the story. You must have been terribly frightened, but you acted so quickly."

"Well, it was a bit... harrowing; but the man is behind bars now. I thought that they would just let him go, but it turns out that he had prior offenses, so hopefully he'll be put away for a while. I'm just trying to put the whole thing behind me." Kursta redirected the conversation, looking over at GP. "We've got ourselves a beautiful horse there, don't we?"

"Yes, I've heard we're partners now. How long have you owned GP?"

"I'm going to take GP back to the paddock so he can be walked," Roman interjected.

Ruby walked up to the horse and gave him one last long stroke, amazed that she actually owned him–well, at least fifty percent.

Kursta responded to Ruby's question. "I've had him since he was a foal. Have you seen his pedigree?"

Ruby shook her head no and looked over at Morgan.

"You'll be getting all his papers when we meet later today." Morgan nodded in reassurance.

"Do you intend to keep your ownership interest in GP?" Kursta asked Ruby point-blank.

"Why don't you give her some time to make that decision," Morgan admonished Kursta.

"I do need some time to figure that out." Ruby wondered how Hilde had fit into the entire horseracing scene.

"He's also sought after as a sire. He has very strong lineage on both sides," Kursta added.

"Did Hilde ever come out to the track to see GP?" Ruby asked.

Morgan responded, "When she first bought him I brought her out to the track a few times. Once in a while they would broadcast a race."

"She loved her GP and she trusted my management, for which I am grateful. I hope that can continue," Owen added.

"My aunt always loved horses. I must admit though, I am a bit surprised she would purchase a racehorse so late in life."

There was a moment of silence.

"People do a lot of things that we don't understand. That's their right. It's called free will." Morgan responded.

"You should tell Ruby about the Bash coming up,

Kursta," Owen changed the subject.

"Bash? What's that?" Ruby asked.

"The Bashes are monthly get-togethers for the owners in the racing commission," Kursta said. "I put them on. Every month they have a new theme. This month's theme is The Great Gatsby. I hope you can join us." Kursta pulled out an invitation from her briefcase and handed it to Ruby.

"It sounds like a good time," Ruby smiled.

"Tell ya what," Owen chimed in. "You said you wanted to learn more about horse racing and what led your aunt to acquire a racehorse. Why don't we go to dinner, I'll tell you all about GP, and then we can go to the Bash together afterwards."

"Wonderful idea!" Kursta put her hands together in a silent clap of joy.

Ruby felt pressured. Did she just get asked out on a date? She looked at Morgan. "Do you ever go to the... 'Bashes'?"

"I am not myself a horse owner, but I have been a guest at a Bash or two. I'm not a big partier, but they are quite an experience." He pressed his lips together.

Ruby agreed to go to dinner and the Bash with Owen, not thoroughly convinced it was a wise decision. She rationalized that she could always cancel if she chickened out last minute. They exchanged contact information and Morgan politely nudged Ruby that it was time to head for their next stop.

Chapter 12

Ruby asked Morgan to stop at her place to get her car before going to Hilde's estate. She decided she would rather drive herself, plus she might decide to stay longer than he wanted.

Standing atop a hill overlooking Tolstoy, 3113 Green Gable Lane offered an unrivaled view much like Morgan's home, but from the other side of town, the west side. The driveway behind the broken off gate was steep and narrow. Once at the top, Morgan pulled his Mercedes around the circular driveway and parked in front of the brick steps leading to the front door of the two-story mansion. Ruby followed suit, pulling her car in behind Morgan's.

Ruby stepped out and waded through a river of weeds to get to the walkway. She dusted off the cobwebs from one of the windows and cupped her hands around her face as she peeked into one. She saw the silhouettes of furniture.

"A long time ago I came to this house for a Christmas party of your aunt's." Morgan looked up at the expanse of the structure. "It was by far the most extraordinary place in the entire county. People were always begging your aunt for a tour of her lovely estate. There were even a couple of magazine and newspaper articles written about it. It's all gone to shit, but with some TLC, it will come back to life."

Morgan fumbled in his front pocket for a set of keys. He produced a ring of assorted shapes and sizes and proceeded to try each one in the front door before coming to the right key. He opened the door and motioned for

Ruby to enter before him.

The air in the house was cool and dank. The decor immediately brought Ruby back to her childhood home. She recognized the red rocking chair in the corner of the living room and rested her hand on the arm, feeling the familiar bristly burnout upholstery.

"My aunt rocked me in this chair."

"She did?" Morgan didn't feign interest well. "It's been a long time since anyone's been in the house," Morgan established, before noticing a far broken window in the dining room. "Maybe not. Looks like there have been some vandals." A dining room chair had been toppled over, and a few shattered glass figurines covered parts of the hardwood floor. He moved in closer to get a better look as he pulled a flashlight from his jacket pocket and pressed it on.

"No one took care of the house at all?" Ruby asked in an indignant tone, since she was now responsible for it.

"There was a gardener for a while but no real caretaker."

"But you were the executor of her will, weren't you? Wasn't it your responsibility to keep it up?"

Morgan laughed, matching Ruby's tone. "She didn't pay me for that. It wasn't part of the contract."

Ruby turned to make eye contact. "So, exactly what was in your contract?"

"My job was to ensure her bills were paid every month and that she was taken care of; and eventually to settle her estate as she intended it to be—with you as her sole heir." Ruby thought the way he worded the statement was curious.

The two proceeded to make their way through the first story of the house with Morgan opening up the curtains and blinds in each room as they went. There was a blanket of dust on everything. Ruby coughed a few times. She simply couldn't believe that as Hilde's executor, Morgan wouldn't ensure her house was taken care of. She became anxious to spend time in the house—once the power was turned on—so she could not only assess all the damage, but also reconnect with memories of her aunt.

In addition to the large formal living room, the downstairs hosted an adjacent, well-sized dining room with a table for ten, a study with built-in cherry book shelves on three sides, an industrial-sized gourmet kitchen with a butler's pantry, laundry room, maid's quarters, and an expansive game room equipped with a snooker table, dartboard, a "Hot Tip" pinball machine, and a long shuffleboard table. A jukebox sat in one corner as well as an upright player piano. From the opposite corner of the room, closest to the window, Ruby saw something red sparkle.

"Hey, look over there." Ruby walked toward the opposite side of the room.

"I'm afraid my eyes can't see as well as yours." He followed her, shining the light in front of her so they could both see well.

The head of a horse seemed to emerge from a wood table in a far dark corner. Ruby walked over to the head. It was black with bright, vermilion nostrils and wild eyes. "It's part of a carousel horse. But, it's only the head."

"I remember that horse. It used to stand by this window." Morgan bent down beside her to get a closer look at it. "Someone sheared it off right at the neck. Now, why in the hell would someone do that? What a shame." The one eye facing them was a red crystal. Ruby looked on the other side of the head. The crystal in that eye was missing.

"Where's the rest of it?" Ruby questioned. Morgan and Ruby scanned the room, but the rest of the body was nowhere to be found. "Isn't a horse head considered a bad omen?"

"You've watched *The Godfather* too many times. Before we go upstairs, I'll show you your aunt's room—the one she stayed in before moving to Meadowview." They walked through the kitchen past the pantry and laundry.

"Are these maid's quarters? She slept in the maid's quarters of all places?"

"It was the only bedroom downstairs. She couldn't climb the stairs anymore." Morgan opened the door to let Ruby go in first.

This room was much brighter from the natural light coming in from a large south-facing window. The furnishings were modest and minimal, shaker style—a twin bed, desk and chair, a small highboy dresser, and an old trunk.

"Meow." An orange tabby announced itself and jumped up on the bed.

"We must have left the front door open," Morgan surmised.

"Cats are a nuisance." Ruby stepped over the cat to get a better look at a silver-framed black-and-white picture on the dresser. "Anyway, I'm allergic."

It was Hildegard, most likely in Africa after Ruby left home. She stood next to a camel, holding it by a halter, in front of a stone structure. She had a huge smile on her face and wore a white-collared linen blouse. It was a superior candid shot, quite Ralph Lauren-esque. Hilde looked like she was smiling right at Ruby, almost saying, "What took you so long?"

"God, your aunt was elegant, wasn't she? She'll always be smiling at you in her eight-by-ten desert." Morgan's words made Ruby ache, longing for her Aunt Hilde; wondering what her later years had been like.

Ruby opened the top drawer of the dresser. Inside lay another picture. This one was of Hildegard, Ruby's mother, and herself. Ruby looked closely at the picture. On the back was written, *Hilde, Grainger, and little Ruby*. She picked it up and showed Morgan, who had picked up the fluffy orange hairball and was now stroking it. The cat purred loudly.

"You have a way with cats. See, here's my mom and my aunt together." Ruby showed Morgan the picture.

"And that's you." Morgan pointed to the little girl in the picture, temporarily pausing the stroking of the cat. The cat nudged his hand to get back to its job.

"Can you tell which one is Hilde?" Ruby asked.

"The one on the left?" Morgan asked.

"Wrong!" Ruby laughed and put the picture down.

"Let me put this cat outside, and then I'll show you the upstairs."

The stairwell was quite beautiful despite the thick coat of dust it had accumulated. It was innately carved in cherry and curved in a 360-degree turn as Ruby reached the top step. Two grimacing gargoyles decorated the wood above the stairs. One stared directly off into space while the other focused down at the would-be ascender. It peered right through Ruby, its eyes seeming to follow her upward movement until coming to a standstill as she reached the second floor.

The top floor of the home held four guest bedrooms, all ensuite—atypical for the era—and one large master bedroom. There was a sitting area at the top of the stairs with a loveseat, two winged-back chairs, and a coffee table, which overlooked the living room below. They peeked into each room but didn't spend much time there. Morgan told Ruby he would need to leave soon. There were no signs of intruders on the top floor. They made their way back downstairs.

"I have some things for you to sign, and then I can turn your aunt's property over to you." Morgan assumed a more professional air. Ruby joined him at one end of the long dining room table as he pulled some papers from his briefcase followed by a black velvet pouch. Morgan reviewed the deed to the house with Ruby as well as GP's lineage papers, the race association contract, and the bank accounts. "All accounts are now in your name."

Ruby pointed to the velvet pouch. "What's that?"

Morgan untied it, loosened the opening, and pulled out the huge, crystal green teardrop. He placed it into

Ruby's hand.

"My God!" Ruby held it up to the light. "I've never seen anything like it in my entire life." Her eyes grew wide as she turned the stone in her hands. "Is it real?" she gulped.

"Yes, it's real. It's estimated at 1.2 million dollars. Here is the GIA study."

"Are you kidding?" Ruby laughed out loud in disbelief. "It's an emerald, right?" she asked, taking a closer look at it.

"No, it's a green diamond, extremely rare. Legend says—or at least rumor has it—that some people have died over this stone. Be sure to safeguard it and be careful in who you show it to."

"I wonder if my aunt got it in Africa."

"There's some information on it in the documents that go along with it."

Morgan changed topics. "You'll need to find a reputable financial advisor who can help you make some solid investments. And you should have a will drawn up for yourself. It's never too early."

"You can help me with that, right?" Ruby asked.

"If you'd like." Morgan stood up from the table, suggesting he was ready to leave.

"You're leaving?" Ruby asked.

He looked at this watch. "Afraid so." Morgan scratched a sagging spot of skin on his throat. He picked up his attaché case and headed for the door. He turned to Ruby.

"Is this goodbye, then?" she asked.

"Call the office and we'll get something scheduled soon."

"Alright, well thanks for everything," Ruby stood up and reached out to Morgan in an awkward hug.

Morgan made his way to the door and then turned around. "Ruby, within these walls, I hope you find yourself reconnected to your aunt and even to your mother. You may learn something about yourself here. You remind me of Hilde in some respects." He took one long last look at the house as he walked out the door, leaving it open. "Don't forget the key's in the door," he called out to her as he left.

Despite the strange goodbye, Ruby found herself quickly absorbed by the green diamond lying beside her on the table. She picked it up and held it to the sunlight coming in from the window. She couldn't believe it was really worth $1.2 million! She pinched herself on the underside of her forearm. She wondered how her aunt had come to own the diamond, and who had lost their lives over the stone. Could it really be true?

Ruby picked up GP's pedigree, and read through the names of his ancestors. She could tell nothing about GP from the names. She did not recognize any of the horses. It was not as if Secretariat or Man O' War was in his bloodline. She was looking forward to her dinner with Owen so she could learn more about GamePlan. As much as she was interested in keeping the horse, she wanted to make sure she was investing her money wisely.

The long creaking sound of a door opening startled Ruby. That stupid cat must have come back. The noise seemed to come from Hilde's room. Ruby quickly tucked the diamond back into its pouch and then into her purse, which she slung over her shoulder. She stood up and froze for a moment. What if it wasn't the cat? Her heart throbbed in her throat.

Ruby heard something fall. Her pulse pounded in her ears, faster now. Her breaths were speeding up. She realized she had no way to call anyone for help. If there was a phone in the house, she was certain the service was not turned on.

"Hello?" She scanned the kitchen for a knife or something she could quickly grab to defend herself. She heard something else topple as she spotted a butcher block full of knives on the counter at the opposite side of the room. "Who's there?!" she repeated herself as she ran quickly to it and pulled out the largest knife as quietly as she could.

She stepped down the hallway back toward Hilde's room, holding the knife at shoulder height, ready to use it. The door was ajar but not open all the way. Ruby kicked it open. She heard a thud. The door handle hit the wall. She looked down and the orange cat swished by her leg, suddenly exiting the room. She looked up and saw Kleptstein standing in front of her. She closed her eyes and screamed at the top of her lungs. She opened her eyes. No one was there. She saw that a picture and vase had toppled over on the dresser.

Ruby turned in a circle quickly, making sure nothing and no one else was in the room. She was ready with the knife just in case. She walked slowly toward the closet and slid the door open. She peaked inside. Nothing.

Had she imagined that Kleptstein was there?

The cat reappeared and jumped up on the bed. Ruby sat down hard beside it, shaking. She couldn't get Kleptstein's face out of her mind. Had he really been there?

The cat jumped onto her lap and started rubbing its head on her chest. She stood up so it would jump to the floor.

Ruby sneezed and suddenly felt an allergy attack coming on. Still shaking, she went back into the dining room. The cat followed her. Ruby dumped the contents of her purse onto the table to find her inhaler. She spotted a Benadryl tablet still in its foil packet. She popped it open and swallowed the pill dry. She found her inhaler in the side pouch of her purse and took a puff. She was shakier than ever. She usually rinsed her mouth out after taking her inhaler to help ward off the shakes, but she couldn't do that here. She just wanted to get home.

She scooped up the contents of her purse, ensuring she had the diamond and the GIA study, then shoved the rest of the documents into her bag as well. She made a mental note to pull the keys out of the front door as Morgan had reminded her.

As Ruby walked out the door, she stopped dead in her tracks. A single red rose had been left on the doorstep.

Chapter 13

Kursta had spent a long day at the racing commission office preparing for the next board meeting, which was going to focus on the state investigation. She was also tying up loose ends for the next Bash. She intended not to leave the office in the dark, but she lost track of time. Hyper-observant, she locked up the office and made her way down the outside stairs to her car. As she approached her vehicle, she realized she hadn't taken out her keys. She began fumbling through her purse at her doorside. She knew she should have dug them out before she left the building. Although she didn't see anyone around, she began to panic. Sandy's voice boomed in her head. His physical presence wasn't necessary to remind her of her debt. Suddenly, her fingers came across the horse head figurine attached to her key chain lurking at the bottom of her bag, and she quickly got into her car. She locked the doors.

Kursta started her car and looked at the backside area of the track in her rearview mirror. In an area lit on the far side of the stables, she spotted Sandy carrying what looked to be a briefcase. He was headed in her direction. Thankful for the safety of her car and some distance, she pulled out of her parking spot and drove for the service gate. She knew it would be closed, but thankfully she had a remote on her visor. She pushed it and felt relieved when the gate slowly began to open. She could still see Sandy in her rearview mirror. He continued to walk in her direction.

She hadn't spotted his truck, but she knew it must be close by. As long as she could get out of the gate, she would be safe—for now.

The gate continued to slowly chug open. Kursta kept her eye on her rearview mirror. She lost sight of Sandy as he went around a building. She figured he would be getting into his pickup and would soon be behind her.

She returned her focus on the gate. It had stopped. It was open more than halfway, but not wide enough for her to get her Volvo through. She pushed the visor remote repeatedly. She looked in her rearview mirror and saw headlights coming toward her. She couldn't tell what kind of car it was, but it was gaining.

The gate re-engaged and began opening again. Kursta was barely able to get her car through. She heard her right-side mirror scrape against the gate. As she took a right onto the frontage road, she could see the car behind her passing through the gate. She just needed to get to the freeway ramp and then could get lost in the traffic. She breathed a sigh of relief as she merged into the current of red taillights.

Twenty minutes later, Kursta pulled into her designated parking spot at her condominium complex. She had complained to the office that the parking lot wasn't well lit, but nothing had been done about it. She would need to escalate it at the next HOA meeting. She grabbed her briefcase and purse out from the backseat and proceeded into the even darker stairwell leading to her second story condo. As she started up the stairs, a burly forearm in a leather jacket pulled her back by her throat.

"I'm here to remind you of a debt you have with the Sandman. You know who I'm talking about, right?" The man's arm remained locked around her neck. Kursta nodded rapidly. She didn't recognize the voice.

"He needs to know your plan."

"My plan?" Her voice was a scratchy whisper.

"Yes, your plan to pay him."

"I'm working on it."

"That's not good enough. You need to tell me your plan right now."

"I'm working on getting the money from my boyfriend."

"Who is he?"

"I don't want to bring him into this."

With his left arm still coiled around her neck like a fat boa constrictor, he took her right hand into his leather glove. She tried to wriggle her hand out of his, but it was no use. He crumpled her hand in his grip like a newspaper. She screamed but he muffled her mouth with the same-gloved hand. Her scream turned into a whimper. Then she began to mumble.

"I'm going to take my hand off your mouth and then you're going to tell me your plan."

Kursta nodded quickly again. The man moved his hand just enough off her mouth to where she could speak and he could understand her.

"I have a plan, but I need to tell Sandy directly about it."

"Fair enough. Let's go visit Sandy. I'll take you now."

Chapter 14

Suki stood behind Ruby and made fish faces in the mirror as Ruby carefully applied a coat of red matte color with a brush to her more-than-usually-plump upper lip—still swollen from her cat encounter.

"You said the theme is The Great Gatsby?" Suki asked. "Your dress is beautiful." Ruby wore a dark blue thirties' style hand beaded gown she found in a vintage store.

"And, I like your necklace." Suki pointed to her own matching necklace in the mirror, the left half of a silver heart with a jagged middle. The word "Best" was engraved in it.

"I love it," Ruby pointed to the right half of the silver heart hanging around her neck with the word "Friends." When the two broken halves were put together, they formed a full heart reading "Best Friends." The necklaces were a gift Suki had bought for them.

"You're doing a lot better. I can tell." Ruby looked at her in the mirror.

Suki nodded and gave her a smile, closing her eyes and showing the gap between her two front teeth.

Within the last week, Suki had started sleeping in the guest bedroom, which was a real improvement. She was starting to joke again and seemed more like herself.

"Hey," Ruby turned away from the mirror so she could make direct eye contact with Suki. "There's something I need to tell you."

"Are you mad at me?" Suki raised her shoulders as if

she were bracing for a blow.

"No. You have to promise to keep everything a secret, OK?"

"Of course."

Ruby could no longer contain what had happened to her at the Green Gable and was ready to tell Suki everything about what she had inherited from Hilde. Ruby was nervous how Suki might take the news. She didn't want Suki to view her any differently. Plus, she was worried that any change to Suki's environment might disrupt the stability she was finally regaining.

"Hilde left me with enough money to where I don't need to work anymore if I don't want to."

"Oh my God!" Suki screamed and put both her hands over her mouth like the Monkey who could speak no evil.

"There's more," Ruby said calmly.

"I also inherited a rare green diamond and an estate. It needs a lot of work."

"I don't think there is such a thing as a green diamond. I think you mean an emerald."

"That's what I thought, too, but I have the paperwork to prove it's a diamond. I'll show it to you tomorrow, but there's more."

Suki's eyes were as big as saucers. "Go on!"

"I have inherited a racehorse. Well, half a racehorse. There is another owner, too. It's Kursta Blithey, that lady that was on the news with Kleptstein. I met her yesterday and that is why I'm going to this party tonight. It's for the horse racing association."

"What half of the racehorse did you inherit?" Suki asked.

"Hopefully, the half that wins! I also inherited a mansion—The Green Gable Estate."

"What?! I know that place! Your aunt owned that mansion?"

"Yes, but it needs so much work. I was there yesterday and something strange happened."

"What do you mean something happened?"

"So, the attorney and I went through the entire house, and then he had to leave to go to an appointment. There was this orange cat in the house. I was there all by myself with the paperwork, the diamond, and everything, and I heard a noise behind the kitchen in one of the bedrooms. Anyway, I heard a door open, so I grabbed a kitchen knife and went back toward the bedrooms and the cat jumped out."

"That would have freaked me out."

"But then I saw Kleptstein's face."

"The creepy rose guy? He was in the house?"

"I screamed and closed my eyes. When I opened them, he wasn't there. He wasn't there. It was just the cat."

"So, was the creepy rose guy there or not?"

"I am not sure."

The doorbell rang.

Ruby and Suki looked at each other. "It's your date."

"Wait. This is the most important thing I have to tell you...When I left the house, there was a single red ruby rose on the doorstep, just like the ones Kleptstein would give me at the club every night."

"No shit?! That's creepy. So was he there?"

"I don't know. He's the only one I know who leaves red roses around."

"You still want to move there?" Suki asked.

The doorbell rang again.

"I gotta go." Ruby ran out of the bathroom to answer the door.

Ruby made a mental note of where she had placed the diamond in its pouch along with all her paperwork in the top drawer of her dresser. She simply had no other place to put it until she could get a safe. She covered it up with some stained panties and made sure her bedroom door was closed—since it didn't have a lock.

"Why do you always have to go when the conversation is just getting good?" Suki followed Ruby into the living room.

Ruby opened the front door.

"Hi, Owen!" Ruby put on a cheerful smile.

"Wow, what an outfit. You look gorgeous!"

"And look at you in that lime green zoot suit!"

"Oh, we will be quite the pair, won't we?" He flashed his white, beautiful smile.

Suki cleared her throat behind them.

Ruby turned toward her. "Owen, this is my roommate and best friend, Suki Giles."

Suki walked up to him and put out her hand. She and Ruby were both surprised when Owen held it up to his mouth and kissed it delicately.

"Enchanté." He was definitely charming.

Suki knelt in an awkward ballet curtsy and fell to the floor. They all laughed.

As Owen walked toward the front door, Ruby looked back at Suki, who gave her an exaggerated wink. Ruby blew her a kiss in customary fashion.

* * *

Owen took Ruby to the Dim Sum Diner, a new four-star Asian fusion restaurant on the west side of town. Ruby sipped a signature cucumber-cilantro martini while Owen gave her a rundown on GamePlan's history.

"Your Aunt Hilde...bless her heart, she was one sweet lady," Owen started. "When I met her, she had just lost her other horse, Kingston, a Preakness winner. He had potential to be a great sire. And that was Hilde's plan. She was devastated, naturally, and said she wanted another horse right away."

The buzzy warmth of the martini helped Ruby focus on Owen's lips, which she decided were perfectly formed.

It was not long and their dinner arrived.

"How did she lose Kingston?"

"He collapsed after a race."

"How terrible. Why did that happen?"

"They never found out for sure. It could have been cardiac arrest. They checked for pulmonary hemorrhaging but there were no signs. He was never quite the same after the Preakness. He ran a few more races, but his times were never the same. The last race was more than he could handle."

"It must have been horrific. I can't imagine what it did to my aunt."

"It was devastating. There is no other way to describe it." Owen paused for a moment to take a drink from his bottle of Tsingtao. "Let's talk about GP." He brightened. "Now, GP had just run a couple of races when half his interest came up for sale. He didn't do so well at first, which is not uncommon for a brand-new racer. A Japanese couple with fifty percent ownership got cold feet and pulled out. Your aunt bought their share. Then, I became his trainer. I had a completely different regimen of training, rest, and supplements than all the other trainers in the region, and I was getting results. When I was in Kentucky, I learned from the best, and I knew GP was going to blossom under my training; and he did. Your aunt was very happy. She told me she never wanted anyone else to train her GP."

Ruby wondered how much of what Owen said she could really believe; but she found herself really enjoying listening to him nonetheless. It didn't seem long that their dinner was over and the dishes were removed.

Owen looked down at his watch. "We need to go."

"So soon?" Ruby would have preferred to stay at the restaurant and hear more about GP. She was a bit nervous about going to the Bash and started a little line of welts on the underside of her forearm with her nails.

"Afraid so, but the night has just begun," Owen flashed Ruby that smile, and stood up to track down their waitress since they hadn't received the check yet.

The pair headed up the windy dirt road to West Shores Way in Owen's Land Rover. Their destination was a warehouse at the top of a cliff. Expensive cars with their lower halves blanketed in dust lined one side of the building. Owen pulled up in front where a young valet greeted them.

"Good evening, Mr. Kierney. Welcome to The Great Gatsby Bash. Park wherever you'd like and we'll show you to your Packard."

Ruby stepped out of the car and straightened out her skirt. The evening wind whipped her hair and dress around her body tightly.

"It's violent out tonight, isn't it?" Owen commented.

A 1933 Packard pulled up behind Owen's car. A gentleman jumped out, opened the backseat suicide door, and helped Ruby inside. Once Owen was inside, the car pulled to the South side of the building and stopped. The driver got out and opened their door.

The front of the building, which was actually the back, had a spotlight on each side of the entryway. A man with a white period sports coat stood behind a stand with a clipboard.

"Good evening, Mr. Kierney."

"Good evening, Max. My guest is Ruby Sans. She's the new owner of GamePlan."

The young man went down a list on his clipboard and checked off their names. "Ms. Sans, welcome to the Bashes. We're featuring Aquarian entertainment and live reptilian art this evening. Your next stop is the hospitality station where they will serve the Evening Initiator." He pointed the way. "Enjoy."

"Evening Initiator?" Ruby turned to Owen.

"There's always a signature drink to get the party started." A young blond woman with a low-cut gold dress and a black pillbox hat flashed Owen a big smile and an ample view of cleavage.

"Owen, you're looking quite dapper tonight."

"Why thank you, Daphne. Let me introduce you to the new co-owner of GamePlan, Ruby Sans."

"Pleased to meet you. I'm so sorry to hear about your aunt."

Ruby responded with an uncomfortable "thank you." How many people knew Hilde?

"Is this your first Bash, Ms. Sans?"

Ruby nodded.

"Our Evening Initiator is a Prohibition Champagne Cocktail." Daphne handed Owen and Ruby each a coupe.

"Bottom's up." Owen shot down his drink and slammed the glass down on the table. Ruby wasn't that fond of champagne but followed his lead, slamming her glass down as well.

"You're going to have the time of your life. These parties are the greatest."

Owen winked at Daphne. "Catch you later."

"Have a good time."

From the hospitality station they walked into a large room. Ruby could see the building was as large and tall as an airplane hangar. She couldn't believe how many people were there. It was very crowded and noisy.

"Owen," an older gentleman called out.

Owen turned to Ruby. "Ruby, I'm so sorry, I need to speak with a business associate for just a few minutes. Have a look around, and I'll catch up with you, OK?"

"OK," she responded.

"I won't be long. I promise."

Ruby walked deeper into the room and could see a crowd of people hovering around a swimming pool. Women with large, muscular thighs and shiny silver bathing caps that reminded her of disco balls did a water dance to a mix of 1930s-era music mixed with repetitive, rhythmic house techno pop. People in thirties-period dress stood watching. Others along the sides danced. Everyone seemed to take the party theme pretty seriously.

A young Asian woman in high heels and a turquoise satin brocade dress with a mandarin collar approached Ruby. "You're new to the Bashes, aren't you?" Ruby noticed that the woman's eyebrows moved in unison with her lashes every time she blinked, like some sort of tic. The woman gave Ruby a once-over, starting with her shoes and moving right up her body to her head.

"Is it that obvious?" Ruby smiled.

"You just look a little...lost. These parties can be a bit overwhelming at first. Are you the new owner of GamePlan?"

"Yes. Everyone seems to know who I am."

"The racing circle is a bit small and incestuous." The woman, who wasn't even five feet tall, stepped closer to Ruby. "You've got a race coming up. Everyone has been waiting to see if your horse can make a comeback. It may be his only chance. He was on fire for a while but hasn't been doing so well under the new trainer."

"You mean under Owen Kierney?"

"Yes. Do you know anything about him?"

"I'm just getting to know him. He brought me here tonight."

"Oh." The woman smiled in disgust. "Yes, he can be quite charming. Watch out. Don't let him charm the pants off you."

Ruby was taken aback. "Wow, this is a lot to take in. I thought GamePlan was racing well."

"Is that what Owen told you, or his precious mommy? GP's on a losing streak. You better read up on his performance. Don't take other people's word for it or they will take advantage of you. That's what they did to your aunt."

"Who is Owen's mother?"

"Only the General Manager of Diamond Head Stables."

"Kursta Blithey?"

"I'm sure you've heard that our former city councilwoman is also a hometown hero..." She formed quotations with her fingers in the air. "Unless you've been under a rock. Underlying message, she's untouchable."

A wave of heat and nausea rose in Ruby's gut. Her

head started pounding.

"Be careful, Girl." The woman blinked her eyes and eyebrows. She pointed her index finger up to the sky, which did a fleeting snake charm dance in unison with her head. "You've entered a whole new world." Her voice was extremely loud now.

Ruby was dizzy. She looked down at the floor a moment to get her bearings. When she looked up again, the woman was gone. Ruby scanned the crowd to see if she could find her. She hadn't caught her name. How could she have disappeared so quickly?

Ruby drifted with the current of the crowd, searching for the woman's aqua-blue dress in the sea of colors. Beads of sweat fell down the back of Ruby's dress. She longed for fresh air and water. She had wandered off so far from Owen, she wasn't sure if she'd find him again.

Ruby eventually found herself in another large room where glass cases housed colorful snakes and lizards. Under each case shone a black light, casting haunting hues on the creatures inside. From the ceiling, lights switched colors rhythmically. The same '30's music but without the house mix weaved through the buzz of conversation. Ruby stood absorbing the visual stimuli around her. For a wave, the colors suddenly intensified and the movement of one of the lizards caught Ruby's attention.

She stared curiously at the texture of its skin. Her usual repulsion by such creatures was suddenly replaced with a queer fascination. She stepped closer to the case and watched the reptile test the boundaries of its glass world. As it paced back and forth, Ruby studied the shadows cast by the different colors in the valleys of its hide. She longed to touch it. She raised her hand to the glass and pressed her fingertips to the flickering tongue.

From behind, someone reached around Ruby and put a hand over her eyes.

"Guess who?"

Startled, she backed off from the cage suddenly.

"Owen?"

He took his hand off of her face.

"Enjoying yourself?"

"No. You left me for a long time. I don't feel well. I need some water and some air."

"Here, sit down." He led her by the hand to a bench next to the wall. "I'll get you some water. I promise I'll only be gone a moment."

Owen returned on his word with a plastic cup filled with water. Ruby downed it in a series of swallows without a breath.

"I'm not—I'm not feeling well." Ruby breathed heavily. "The colors are hurting my eyes. And I'm really hot. Please take me outside." She brushed her hair out of her face.

"Here, let's get some air." Owen put an arm around Ruby and headed toward a side exit.

"You'll be feeling fine in no time."

Owen pushed the door open, which led to an outdoor atrium. He sat Ruby down on a marble bench, steadying her shoulders.

"How are you now?"

Ruby looked down at the cement, then back up to Owen. "I don't feel like I'm in a real place."

"It's good to step out of reality once in a while and let yourself be and see anything you want to." The volume of his voice was turned down to a whisper. "Ruby. Allow yourself to live a lifetime in a moment." She wasn't sure what he meant by that. On second thought, perhaps he didn't say that at all.

Owen's voice suddenly shifted and seemed to come from a muted megaphone in the distance, but she couldn't make out what he was saying. His face was right above hers, looming like the big shiny moon she'd spotted earlier. Ruby could make out a single saxophone playing *Harlem Nocturne* in the distance. Was she really hearing it, or was it in her head? She thought she must be on the ground now. The full moon above her rotated and then swirled faster and faster like a balloon losing helium. It grew smaller and smaller until finally fading into black on the final note of the song.

Chapter 15

Ruby blinked several times. Her focus was fuzzy, and the side of her head felt like it had been hit with a shovel.

"Good morning," she heard a man's voice say.

"Where am I?" She put her hand up to feel the lump above her ear. The hair was matted over what felt like half a golf ball she could barely stand to touch. A wave of panic flooded her. What had happened? What had she done?

"You're at my place." Fingers waved in front of her. "It's Owen."

Ruby bolted up into a sitting position and immediately vomited all over herself. She looked down at the vomit covering her bra and the velour blue blanket that had been spread over her. She looked around to get a sense of her surroundings, but moving her eyes made her feel even more nauseated.

"I'll get a towel. Stay put." Owen came back and smeared a towel over Ruby awkwardly. Her eyes began to clear up. "I need to get to a bathroom."

Owen helped her to her feet and held her arm as he guided her down the hall. Ruby leaned forward and grabbed for the doorframe.

"I've got it. I've got it!" She closed the door behind her and locked it. "Oh my God, what happened?!" She winced as she faced the mirror. The lump on the side of her head protruded with dried blood plastering her hair to her head. There was also a small streak of dried blood in front of her ear.

"You had a bit of a spill at the party... You fell outside in the atrium and hit your head," Owen projected his voice through the door.

"I'm taking a shower. Where are your towels?"

"Under the sink. Do you want company?"

"Company?" Ruby thought to herself. She suddenly remembered her conversation with the Asian woman the night before. Had Owen charmed the pants off her?

"I mean help."

"No! No company, no help." She double-checked the lock on the door and peeled off her soiled bra and panties.

"Where's my dress?" she called. Owen didn't respond. He must have walked away from the door.

She reached down to pull a towel out from under the sink as her pulse pounded in her ears. She felt dizzy as she stood up and thought she might vomit again. False alarm.

She turned on the shower and waited for the water to warm up. She was thirsty beyond belief. She tried to remember the last thing that happened the night before. The last thing she could recall was the reptiles in their glass cases and how hot it was in the room.

She stepped into the now adequately hot water and let it run over the back of her head and ever so slightly toward the lump. It stung very badly. She looked down at her feet to see the blood from her head mix with the water. She watched as it turned from brownish red to an eventual yellow and then clear. She washed herself with a bar of soap she found on the side of the tub, turned off the water, and dried herself. She wrapped herself in a towel.

She cracked the door. "Can I borrow some clothes... please?" she called out from the bathroom.

"Are you feeling better?" Owen handed her one of his t-shirts and some athletic shorts. "I'm sure they'll be big. Here, have some Advil." He handed her two brown pills and a glass of water. "You should probably put some ice on your head. I'll get an ice pack."

Ruby emerged from the bathroom a few minutes later,

her stomach twisted in knots from all she didn't know about the night before. She made her way back to what she assumed was Owen's living room. He was on the phone.

"Yes, she's fine," Owen said to the person on the other end. "I've gotta go." He put down the receiver and glanced over at Ruby. "That was my mom."

"Your mom is Kursta Blithey, right?" Ruby eased herself down onto the camel colored upholstered couch.

"That would be her. She was calling to see if you were OK."

"She knew what happened?"

"Everyone at the party knew what happened."

"Really, everyone? There were over a hundred people there." Ruby squinted her eyes, as the light still hurt them. "Why didn't she introduce herself as your mother when I met her?"

"We try to keep it to business at the track. Your attorney is my mom's on-again, off-again boyfriend. Did you know that?"

"No."

"Does it really matter?" Owen asked.

"I suppose not," Ruby said; but somehow, it did matter.

"Look right here." Changing the subject, Owen brought the newspaper over to Ruby and stood over her. He pointed to an article with a picture of a horse crossing a finish line with another not far behind. "The odds for your GamePlan are three to one, can you believe that? They are expecting a record turnout for this week's race. There's a lot of people's money riding on your horse."

Ruby vaguely remembered the conversation with the Asian woman in the water-colored dress. She thought she remembered the woman saying that GP was not running well. While Ruby wanted to explore that topic more, she was more concerned about what else may have happened the night before.

"Tell me what happened last night."

Owen set the paper down on the end table at the end of the couch and sat on an ottoman facing her. He seemed to give her his full attention, looking directly into her eyes. He took a long breath through his nose. "You weren't feeling well after the amphibian and reptile exhibit, so I gave you some water and took you outside to the atrium. We sat on a bench and talked for a little while. I turned my head for a second, and when I did, down you went. I tried to break your fall, but you still hit your head."

"Obviously. You didn't take me to the hospital?"

"It didn't seem that bad. It didn't look like you needed stitches. I was able to stop the bleeding. I put an icepack on your head when we got home."

"Why didn't you take me home to my house? My roommate was home."

"I didn't know she was going to be home and thought someone better watch after you. Plus, I couldn't take you home in your condition. Whether you know it or not, I was up with you all night, making sure you were still breathing and didn't choke on your own vomit. You went through all my clean towels. I barely know you. I would hope I would get a thank you instead of an interrogation. So, I have a question for you."

"What's that?" Ruby wanted more than anything to go home.

"Does this happen often?"

"What?"

"Do you drink until you black out? Has this happened before?"

Who was he to question her like this? "No, I barely drink."

"Really. Could have fooled me. Do you remember anything else about the evening?"

"I think I was drugged."

"You think I drugged you?"

"I'm not saying that you did it. I didn't feel normal after drinking the Evening Initiator. What did they put in it? Some sort of hallucinogenic?"

"I drank the Prohibition Cocktail, too. I felt perfectly fine afterwards. Lots of people—just about everyone—had it. You were the only one who passed out."

"Can you take me home, please? Where's my dress and shoes?"

He looked around by his feet and spotted the navy colored sandals behind the ottoman.

"Here are your shoes."

Ruby noticed they had scuffs on them as he handed them to her.

"As for your dress...it's a mess. You could probably tell by your underwear that it needs to be dry-cleaned. I'm going to the cleaners this week. I'll get it back to you."

There was no emotion in Owen's voice, making it difficult to read him. Ruby wished she could piece more of the night together. She wished she knew if she could trust him. "Can you please take me home now?" She couldn't wait to get out of there.

"Yeah, I'll grab my keys and we can go."

The ride home was long and awkward. The more Ruby stewed on the little she remembered from the night before, the angrier she became. As soon as Owen pulled his car up to the house, she was out. She could barely bring herself to thank him for the ride. He definitely had lost some of his charm. She noticed he didn't waste any time pulling away after she slammed his car door.

Suki's car was in the driveway. Her self-defense class must have been canceled, which was bad news. That meant Ruby could look forward to being interrogated for not coming home last night.

She trudged up the walkway barefoot in Owen's t-shirt and shorts, carrying her heels and dreading what she would face when she opened the door. She was kind of surprised Suki hadn't already spotted her from the window, opened the door and pelted her with questions.

As Ruby put her key into the door, she noticed it wasn't

locked. That wasn't like Suki at all. The TV was blaring. She could hear it through the door.

"Suki?" she called over the loudness of the TV so as not to startle her.

Ruby spotted the TV remote on the end table next to Suki's glasses. It was odd she was not wearing them by now. Ruby reached for the remote and turned it off.

"Suki?"

A chill overcame her as she took a moment to really notice the house. The drawers in the end tables on either side of the couch were open. Where she was standing, she could see into the kitchen where all the cabinets were exposing their contents; same for the drawers. Someone other than Suki must have been in the house. Her heart started racing now. The house was silent.

She turned into the hallway. A slow, steady drip came from the bathroom, killing the silence. It was landing on water, making a bloop sound with each drop. The bathroom door was ajar. Ruby kicked it open all the way. Her chill turned into horror as she saw a bluish foot with pink painted toenails hanging over the side of the tub.

"Sukiiiiiiiiiiiiiii!" Ruby screamed. She pulled back the shower curtain. Suki's face lay a few inches under the surface of the water. Her eyes were staring up, rolled slightly back. Her neck was darkly bruised. Ruby pulled Suki's head out of the water by her pink hair and started hitting her between her shoulder blades in case there was any life left in her. Some water gurgled out of Suki's mouth, but she was stiff. It was too late. She let go of Suki's hair and Suki slid back into her submerged repose. Hyperventilating, Ruby ran into the living room to find the portable phone.

"Nine-one-one, what is your emergency?"

"My friend is dead." Ruby started seeing spots like she did at Hilde's Rosary. That disconnected feeling started creeping in. She knew she had to stay focused. "I found her in the bathtub. It looks like she's been strangled.

She's blue. I tried to pull her out and hit her on the back to get the water out of her lungs, just in case she was still alive, but she didn't respond. I think she's been there for quite some time." Ruby moved into the hallway and stood outside the bathroom, trembling.

"What's the temperature of the water?" the dispatcher asked.

"Umm..." Ruby had to think about it. "It was cool, not warm. I wasn't here last night. I don't want to go back in the bathroom."

"It's all right. We'll send paramedics and an officer right away."

Ruby was shaking uncontrollably. A knot instantaneously formed in her stomach and emptied itself into her mouth. She ran to the kitchen and unloaded it in the sink. She wiped her mouth off with a dishtowel on the counter beside her.

She started pacing through the house. Her bedroom door was open as well as all her dresser drawers. She checked the top drawer. The diamond was gone as well as the GIA study— her fear confirmed. She proceeded to Suki's room. It appeared the intruder had gone through the entire house. Ruby went back into the living room and sat on the couch until the paramedics and police arrived.

"I'm Detective Niver and this is my partner, Detective Mellon." The two police investigators had entered the house, finding Ruby curled in a ball on one end of the sofa, with her head in her hands. Two paramedics followed. She got up and showed the four men to the bathroom, sobbing.

They asked her to wait in the living room while they investigated the bathroom. They searched the entire house and took fingerprints.

One officer walked over to Ruby. "It looks like you hit your head. Was there a struggle?"

"It happened last night. I fell."

"Here? With your roommate?"

"No, I was out last night. I didn't stay here."

"So, she was alone? As far as you know?"

"Yes, I just called nine-one-one as soon as I found her this morning."

Ruby told the detectives when she had last seen Suki as well as how she had found the condition of the house and Suki when she returned. She told them the diamond and accompanying GIA study were missing, and how much the diamond was worth. She also told them everything about how her life had been recently turned upside down with her mother and aunt's deaths, and her inheritance. She believed the diamond was the reason the house was broken into, and the reason Suki was dead.

While interested in what Ruby had to say and thanking her for her opinion, the detectives stated that the evidence would reveal what really happened. They kept turning the conversation to Suki, and rightly so. They asked Ruby to repeat how she found Suki, the position of her body, and everything she had touched since entering the house.

They asked if Ruby knew of any fights or disagreements that Suki had had with anyone lately—a boyfriend, perhaps. Ruby told them what Suki's ex had done to her and that she was letting Suki stay with her until she found another place.

The paramedics checked out Ruby's head and one of the detectives took a picture of it. When Ruby asked why, he said they wanted it since it had happened within the same twenty-four-hour period as Suki's death. It didn't make sense to Ruby, but the detectives assured her it was just part of their time sequencing of events. They wasted no time in wrapping police tape around the fence of the enclosed yard and the front door. They told Ruby to grab a few belongings and assigned a Chaplain to pick her up and drive her to the Hotel Meridien. She was given explicit instructions not to leave town.

Chapter 16

The Hotel Meridien was a historic hotel in the middle of town. The room was comfortable enough, but Ruby could find no comfort. She turned on the news but couldn't watch it. They showed Suki's body bag being wheeled out of the house over and over again. How could those vultures?! Wasn't there anything else worth reporting? She turned off the TV. She figured she should call her landlords and let them know what was happening. Perhaps then they wouldn't be so keen on evicting her. Ruby was sure there were a lot of things she should be doing, but she didn't know what they were. She called Morgan's office.

"I just heard what happened on the radio. Are you all right?" Sydney's voice cracked a bit when she asked the question.

"No, no I'm not. I don't know what to do." Ruby told her the green diamond had also been stolen. "Mil is out of the office until tomorrow, but I will call him at home and let him know you need to speak to him urgently. I'll also book you at nine a.m. tomorrow in case you're not able to connect with him today. Take care, and please let me know if there is anything you need. Be safe."

Be safe? The words were both frightening and validating. The police had little compassion and offered her no protection. When she asked if they thought she could be in danger, they said the crime was most likely targeted at the victim. They did not indicate whether they thought the diamond was the motive of the killing. But, who would want to kill sweet Suki—besides Armando Lewis?

Ruby wondered if she should have checked into the hotel under another name. The hotel phone in her room rang. She decided not to answer it, but to let the hotel's message system pick it up. A minute later, the red message light blinked.

Ruby sat on the edge of the bed watching the light blink on and off. She finally picked up the receiver of the hotel phone and pushed the message play button.

She didn't recognize the voice. "Hey Ruby, this is Travis Benton, your new brother." He chuckled. "I work at Restless Records across the street from Hotel Meridien and I just saw you go in. I'm not trying to stalk you, but I was really happy to see you because I called your house number a couple of times but your answering machine is full. Anyway, I just wanted to talk to you and hope everything is OK with you. Please call me or you can come by the record store. I am here almost every day. OK, hope to hear from you soon."

Ruby decided to walk across the street to the record store where Travis worked. She needed to talk to someone. When she walked in the door, he was sitting behind the counter on a stool eating a sandwich. There was no one else in the store. There were six rows of records separating the two of them.

"Hey, Ruby!" Travis said with his mouth half full and walked around the counter to give her a hug.

Ruby started sobbing.

Travis finished chewing and wiped his hands on his jeans. He put his hands squarely on Ruby's shoulders and looked into her face.

"What's wrong? No offense, but you look like a mess. Did you hit your head?" He inspected the knot on the side of her head.

Ruby nodded yes. "I was at a party last night and passed out and hit my head. I ended up staying the night at this guy's house. I came home this morning and found my roommate dead in the bathtub. She was strangled. Drowned."

"Is this a true story? Oh my God!" Travis held Ruby again and let her sob for a moment into his shirt. "Do you have any idea who it could be?" he asked.

"No. My house is a crime scene so I have no place to stay. That's why I checked into the Meridien."

"Well, I would say you could stay at my place, but you wouldn't want to stay with my roommates. They're pigs. Plus, I'm actually looking for another place to live myself." He paused for a moment. "Ruby, do you think you might be in danger? Do you know of anyone who may be after you?"

Ruby looked at him blankly.

"I'm not trying to scare you, but do you think the person who killed your friend was really after her? What if they were mistaken, and were actually trying to kill you?"

"I don't know."

"And you don't really seem like the type to drink until you pass out."

"It's never happened before."

"I'm a guy who trusts his gut, and I think you need to protect yourself. It's a good thing you're staying at the hotel. It gets a lot of traffic. Stay in public areas. Don't go anywhere alone. You know where I am."

"Thanks, Bro." Ruby said, punching him playfully on the arm. "I'll stay in touch. I better get back to the hotel. My attorney may be calling."

* * *

Sydney had been trying to get in touch with Morgan all day. It was true that he had taken the day off, but she knew he wasn't scheduled to be anywhere. He said he was going to do some things around the house, and it wasn't like him not to answer the phone. Sydney remembered the last time this happened, and it wasn't good. She decided to undertake the thirty-minute drive to his house to check up on him.

The time before, Sydney had taken it upon herself to drive to Morgan's house after a morning of missed appointments and angry clients. She hadn't known what to say to the first two. While Sydney was good with machines and schedules, she was not skilled at making excuses for people. She'd locked up the office before the third client walked up the steps, slipped out the back door, hopped into her car, drove to the other side of town, used the new gate code she'd overheard Morgan mention in a recent phone call, pulled up to his house, and knocked on the door. It pushed open easily, not being closed all the way. She'd searched the house and found Morgan on his kitchen floor in cardiac arrest.

Sydney thought about calling Kursta to see if she knew where Morgan was, but thought better of it. She knew the pair had been on the outs and that Morgan was slowly wiggling out of their relationship. Kursta would ask a lot of probing questions, and Morgan would end up being upset with Sydney.

When Sydney arrived at Morgan's door this time, it was locked. She peered through the windows and heard something—a TV or radio, perhaps. His car was in the garage. She rang the doorbell. After fifteen minutes she picked the lock.

Everything was in its place. She called out for Morgan. Her heart started pounding. She called again, very loudly. There was no answer. She walked into the living room. The television was on. She turned it off and called Morgan's name again. Her breath sped up. Where would she find him this time?

She searched all the rooms, one by one. He was nowhere to be found. She went into the office last. She stopped in her tracks when she saw what was on his desk—a green diamond just like the one Ruby had described as stolen from her house. It had to have been the same one Sydney had seen pictures of in the Tanenbaum file at the office.

Shaking and trying to make sense of why the diamond was on Morgan's desk, she made a beeline for the front door. As she reached for the handle, the door swung open and almost clocked her in the head.

"Sydney! You're in my house. Why are you here?"

Her heart was racing. She could barely hear anything but her heartbeat in her ears. She flung her arms around him. This was very uncharacteristic of Sydney. Morgan patted her arms awkwardly as a sign both that he cared and that she should let go.

"Something terrible has happened." Sydney looked up at him with her arms at her sides now. "I've been trying to call you all day. Ruby Sans' roommate was killed last night. When she got home this morning, the house was torn apart and she found her roommate dead. She's checked into the Meridien Hotel."

"I will call her right away." Sydney could see that he was genuinely concerned.

"I scheduled her for tomorrow at nine a.m."

"That may not be necessary. I'll call her and let you know if we need to keep the appointment."

"I was worried about you. I've had to come here before when you haven't answered your phone, and it wasn't good."

"I know. I have been over at the neighbors' down the hill helping them mend their fence. Their mare got out again." Morgan paused for a moment. "How did you get into my house? I locked the door."

"The door pushed open. Like last time."

Sydney grabbed the door handle and jiggled the knob as if she were trying to find the source of the problem. "I'm glad you're OK, Mil. You're going to call Ruby, right? At the hotel?"

"Yes, right away."

"OK, I know she will want to hear from you. I'll see

you tomorrow." Sydney walked quickly but casually to her car wondering how her boss might be connected to the murder of Suki Giles.

Chapter 17

The phone rang in Ruby's room. She picked it up and gave a reluctant "hello."

"It's Sydney. I found Morgan at home. He's OK. He's going to call you."

"He already did."

"Oh. That was fast. Did he say anything about your diamond?"

"Well, I told him it was missing. He seemed worried, but of course, that's not of primary importance. Finding Suki's killer is."

"Have you thought the two may be connected?"

"Yes, that's all I can think about." Ruby sniffed, obviously crying. "What if my having the diamond led to Suki's murder?"

"I am concerned about you, Ruby."

Ruby was silent for a moment. "I'm going to be OK."

"No, you don't understand," insisted Sydney. "There's something I need to tell you... in person. I don't want to talk about it over the phone."

"Come to my hotel. I'm in Room three-oh-six."

Sydney knocked on Ruby's door twenty minutes later. Ruby let her in and promptly locked the deadbolt and chain.

"What happened to you?" Sydney's eyes grew wide as she saw the bump on Ruby's head. She also noticed Ruby was quite disheveled, wearing a wrinkled t-shirt and cargo pants with a stain on the front.

"I fell at the Racing Association party." Ruby sat down slowly on the bed. "Have a seat." She gestured toward the only chair in the room.

"You went to the Bash?" Sydney seemed to scowl as she set her leather drawstring purse down at her feet and settled as far back as the shallow chair would allow.

"I did." Ruby sighed, perceptibly showing she didn't want to discuss the topic further.

"By yourself?"

Ruby folded her arms and proceeded to pinch the underside of her arm. She didn't like the questions.

"I'm sorry, I don't mean to pry," Sydney explained. "It's just that over the years I've learned a lot about the seedy underbelly of the racing circle. I'm sure you know Morgan's girlfriend is the General Manager at the track. She's not exactly the most scrupulous person. Rumor has it that she's been connected to a few racehorse deaths."

"What do you mean?" Ruby's mind drifted to GamePlan and the upcoming race.

"Let's just say if a horse is not racing well, sometimes it's best to cash out on the policy rather than to put the animal out to pasture." Sydney pursed her lips without the slightest emotion. She reached into her purse and grabbed a tube of lip gloss.

"How do you know so much about it?" Ruby asked.

"Like I said, I've learned a lot working for Morgan all these years, but that's not what I came here to talk about." Sydney glossed her lips and tossed the tube back into the bag. She turned her gaze to Ruby. "You said Morgan didn't say anything about the diamond when he called."

Ruby waited for Sydney to get to the point. "That's right. Why?"

Sydney stood up and reached into the pocket of her hound's-tooth trousers. She pulled her hand out and opened her palm to reveal the green gem.

"How did you get that?" Ruby gasped.

Sydney allowed Ruby to take it out of her hand. "If I

tell you, you must swear to tell no one."

"Do you know who killed Suki? Tell me!" Ruby demanded, putting the diamond in the pocket of her cargos.

"No, I don't know! But you must swear to me that you will keep this a secret, at least for now. You need to trust me. I know you don't know me, but I have no reason to lie to you."

Ruby stared at Sydney for a moment and finally nodded her head in agreement.

"It was on Morgan's desk."

"In his office?!"

"At his house. I drove there today since he wouldn't return my calls. It sounded like the TV was on and he wouldn't answer the door, so I let myself in."

"What do you mean, let yourself in?"

Sydney ignored the question. "I searched the entire house and couldn't find him."

"You broke into his house?"

"Let's just say Morgan has a history. I've had to go find him there a couple of times in the past. When he had his heart attack three months ago, and before that, after his younger brother Jamie committed suicide. I've saved Morgan's ass twice now. I'm a legal secretary. That is not in my job description. He owes me."

Ruby waited for Sydney to continue.

"Turns out, he was at his neighbors'. We ran into each other just as I was leaving the house."

"As you were leaving the house. So he knew you broke in?"

"Like I said, I didn't break in. It wasn't like that. I was worried about him and had to come find him."

"Did you say anything about the diamond?"

"Of course not."

"So, he didn't know you took it? It's just a matter of time and then he's going to come after you."

Sydney swallowed hard. "Mil would never do anything

to hurt me. I know that for certain. Plus, he knows he's not supposed to have the diamond, so why would he say anything about it at all?" She paused for a moment. "You know what this means, don't you?"

"That Morgan killed Suki? Why would he do that? If he didn't want me to have the diamond, he could have simply kept it for himself."

Sydney looked at Ruby not knowing what to say.

"Morgan asked me to come in tomorrow morning at nine." Ruby rolled the diamond between her fingers in her pocket.

"Hmm, he told me he probably didn't need the meeting with you."

"That's not what he said. He insisted that I come in. He said he wouldn't charge me. He just wanted to talk. To make sure I was OK."

"Are you going to come in?" Sydney asked.

"Yes," Ruby took a deep breath. "You will be there, right?"

Sydney nodded. When she left, Ruby put the diamond in a zippered pocket in her purse.

* * *

The next morning, Sydney came into the office at her usual seven thirty. Ruby showed up ten minutes before nine.

"He's not here yet?" Ruby said in a low voice, leaning on the counter above Sydney's desk.

"No. I've given it more thought and think you should call the police after all. Tell them about the diamond. I know I shouldn't have taken it but it's rightfully yours."

"Good morning, Ladies." Morgan came in from the back of the building. Sydney flinched slightly and turned her chair around to him.

"Good morning," the women responded in unison.

"Ruby, come on back to my office."

The women made brief wide-eyed contact as Ruby turned to follow Morgan into his office.

Ruby emerged from Morgan's office about fifteen minutes later.

"Thank you, I will make sure I stay in contact with the police. And by the way, I will be moving into my aunt's estate," Ruby announced. "I can't go back to that house where Suki died." Ruby studied Morgan's face for a reaction.

"It's completely understandable," he responded. "You can restore it back to its former glory. I'd love to see it when it's finished."

Morgan said goodbye and retreated to his office.

"You take care," Sydney said loudly enough for Morgan to hear then mouthed silently to Ruby, "Call me later."

As Ruby closed the door behind her, Sydney realized she was alone in the building with Morgan. She busied herself with some filing that had stacked up over the course of the last week. She hoped that the phone would ring to kill the silence, but it didn't.

Two hours went by without Morgan leaving his private office. The building was as silent as a tomb except for the toilet and the grandfather clock announcing their presence every fifteen minutes or so. It was not like Morgan to stay holed up like that. Sydney started looking at the following day's schedule so she would be prepared with the client files.

As she closed one of the file drawers, Morgan intercommed Sydney. She jumped.

"Sydney, come down to my office." There was no request just an order, and no indication of what he needed.

"I'll be right there. Do I need to bring a Steno pad?"

"That won't be necessary."

Sydney hung up the phone and stood up. She was dizzy, and her heart was pounding loudly in her ears. She started humming a made-up song as she undertook the long walk down the hall to Morgan's office. It was longer than ever before. The door was closed. She knocked before she opened it.

"Sydney, have a seat." He motioned to the chair like she was a client.

She gulped and gave him a big smile in attempt to crack the wall of tension between them. He did not reciprocate.

"Sydney, I need to know the real reason why you were at my house yesterday."

"I told you, I was worried about you and I needed to tell you about what happened to Ruby's roommate."

"I know there was another reason why you broke into my house."

She snapped on the word broke. "Broke into your house? May I remind you that I've saved your life twice now. You never accused me of breaking into your house when you had your heart attack and I had to call nine-one-one. What about that time after Jamie died? You almost lost three clients. You didn't think I was breaking in and entering then."

"The last time you came into my house, I did have a problem with the door; and it did push open rather easily. However, since that time, I had the door relocked. And look what I found in my carpet." He held up a slender picklock tool in a plastic baggy. "Shall I have your fingerprints compared to the ones found on this little instrument?"

Sydney said nothing.

"The other two times you entered my house, I was grateful that you did. You did indeed save my life and a few clients. However, yesterday you stole from me, and I want the item back."

"What do you think I took from your house?"

"We both know what you stole."

"I have no idea what you're talking about." She glanced down at her lap for a moment and then met his gaze. "If you think I stole something from your house, why haven't you called the police?"

"I would hope that wouldn't be necessary. You and I

have worked together a long time. We have built a lot of trust between us."

"Like I said, if you believe I've stolen from you, please report it to the police."

"You don't need a police record, Sydney. I'm going to do something else."

"What's that?"

"Fire you."

Chapter 18

Ruby asked Travis if he'd like to see Hilde's estate. He seemed really happy she asked. He picked her up after she got off work, showing up on his shiny Indian motorcycle. As she gave him a wave hello, she wondered how he could afford such a nice bike working at a record store.

"Who's that guy on the bike?" Jesse, one of Ruby's coworkers who handled the birds of prey, asked as they walked out of the building together. "You got a man now?"

"He's my brother!" She slapped his arm with the back of her hand.

Travis was ready with a helmet for her and opened up one of the leather saddlebags attached to the back of the bike to hold her purse.

"I've never ridden on a motorcycle before," Ruby admitted.

"Piece of cake. Lean when I tell you to lean, but not too far; and hold on tight."

Ruby knew the ride to the Green Gable Estate was going to be a fun one, with the curves leading up to the big hill. She couldn't wait to get there. The estate house utilities were now on and in her name, and she had hired a company to go in and do a thorough cleaning of everything, including the carpets and all the furniture. This would be the first time she'd set foot in the house since the work had been done. She planned to cut back her hours at the Conservatory to do more work on the estate house, so she could move in. She was tired of staying at the Meridien.

Travis maneuvered the bike around the circular driveway to the front steps. He shut it off, set the kickstand, and pulled off his helmet. He could see Ruby needed assistance with her helmet and helped her with the chinstrap.

"So, what did you think of the ride?" Travis combed his fingers through his dark, wavy hair.

"That was awesome!" Ruby beamed.

Travis handed Ruby her purse and she dug her keys out. She remembered the diamond was still in her purse. She opened the door and turned on the lights. The entryway and living room were brightly lit.

"This place is huge!" Travis spread his arms out in a big stretch. "You could fit two of my apartments just in this room!"

Ruby couldn't wait to show the entire house to her brother, especially the game room, like they were a couple of kids. She had hired a handyman to repair the broken window and perform some other minor fixes around the house.

In going through the detached garage, the handyman reported that he discovered the wooden body of the horse. Morgan hadn't bothered to show Ruby the garage when he gave her the tour. The horse head still stood atop the table in the corner of the room.

"This is an old carousel horse." Travis inspected the carving of the mane and the face.

"You know something about carousel horses?" Ruby was surprised.

"Before I worked in the record store, I worked at Jose's Antiques. We had a few carousel horses. We had one similar to this, the same time period. After the Depression they stopped making them entirely out of wood. Now they make them out of fiberglass."

"Do you know why someone would have cut the head off?" Ruby asked.

"Let's carry the head out to the garage where the body

is to take a closer look."

The horse head was heavy, but Travis was able to manage it on his own. Ruby opened the garage door and turned on the light. Travis set the head down on the cement floor next to the body.

"When they sawed off the head, they actually cut into the torso." He picked up the body with the legs connected and turned the torso up on one end so Ruby could see the cut. "Do you see how the body is hollow inside?"

"Yes," Ruby nodded. "It looks like someone cut it open to see if there was something inside the body."

"Exactly. Do you know what Hilde would have hidden inside?" Travis asked.

"No, but I think in time, we'll find out."

"It's a shame they mutilated it." Travis set the body down next to the head. "This is a nice example of a prancer."

"I'm going to have it restored," Ruby declared.

"You know, I'd be interested in doing the work. I still stay in touch with Jose. I'm sure he could put me in touch with an expert so that I do it right and restore it back to its original condition as much as possible. Unless you prefer to have it restored by a professional."

"I'd be happy for you to do it."

"I'll probably have to work on it here, if you don't mind. It would be hard to get it on the back of my bike."

"Or in the back of my Karman Ghia," Ruby laughed.

"I can get started on it this week if you'd like," Travis suggested.

Back in the house, Ruby challenged Travis to a game of pinball on the "Hot Tip" machine.

"So, I take it you're serious about moving into this place." Travis asked Ruby as he launched the pinball into the game.

"Yes, I am. I can't go back to my old place; not after what happened."

Ruby heard a phone ring in the living room.

"You had the phone turned on, too?" Travis turned to her.

"Yes, I was able to keep my same number, but everyone knows to call me at the hotel. Take my turn." Ruby headed for the living room as the phone rang again. She increased her speed. She picked up the handset.

"Hello?"

"Ruby?" It was a woman's voice, vaguely familiar. She sounded like she'd been crying.

"This is Audrey Giles, Suki's mom. I've been trying to get ahold of you. I keep calling your number, but no one answers and it doesn't let me leave a message."

"I'm so sorry. I've been staying at a hotel while the police conducted the investigation."

"Are you back at the house now?"

"No, I had the phone forwarded to a new house. I can't go back there. Are you doing OK?"

"You found her, didn't you?" Suki's mother asked.

The image of Suki's face staring up from below the surface of the water flashed in Ruby's head.

Travis walked in from the other room.

"Yes," was all Ruby could manage to say. Then she started shaking and sobbing. Travis put his arm around her.

"We are having a memorial service for her," Suki's mom said. "Ruby, I hope you can make it."

Chapter 19

The night before Suki's memorial, Ruby agreed to have a drink with Sydney at the Hotel Meridien bar.

"I admit, I didn't see it coming." Sydney stirred her long island tea with a straw.

A small band was setting up to play, which reminded Ruby of Curiocity and how Suki would give her a wink when she glanced over at her in the middle of a song. Ruby's mind drifted off for a moment, wondering if she would ever sing professionally again.

"You OK?" Sydney leaned to make eye contact with Ruby again.

Ruby snapped to. "Yeah, sorry. Everything is reminding me of Suki." She found her place back in the conversation. "Morgan wouldn't have fired you if he didn't feel threatened by you." Ruby took a sip of her Cosmo.

"I suppose you're right."

"Tell me something. Why did you take the diamond to begin with? You could have easily just left it on his desk. Why did you risk so much to give the diamond back to me?"

Sydney looked at Ruby as if she were from another planet. "It was the right thing to do, wasn't it?"

Over Sydney's shoulder, Ruby spotted Detective Niver entering the lobby. "It's one of the detectives." Ruby took a deep breath and forgot to exhale for a moment. She climbed off her barstool and walked his way to meet him, her purse slung over her arm.

She returned to the table a few minutes later. "The detectives want me to come down to the police station. They found the GIA study in one of the bushes in the back yard."

"GIA study? What's that?"

"It's a certificate of authenticity that identifies the diamond."

"You better go then." Sydney proceeded to suck down the rest of her drink. "I'll catch up with you later."

"Not so fast." Ruby locked eyes with Sydney. "They want you to go in, too."

Sydney glanced over to the detective who was watching them patiently from a distance. "You told him that I...?" There was no need to finish the question.

At the police station, Ruby and Sydney were shown to a private room with a tinted window they couldn't see through—just like in the detective TV shows. Ruby wondered if someone was watching on the other side. It didn't really matter to her, but it could matter to Sydney. Officer Mellon entered the room with Niver following behind.

The detectives asked to see the diamond. Ruby unzipped a pouch in her purse and handed it to Officer Mellon. He said he would give it to an analyst to match with the diamond referenced in the GIA study. He asked Sydney where she got the diamond.

"I found it in my former boss' home," Sydney explained.

"So, you stole this from your boss." Detective Niver stated matter-of-factly, holding the gem up to the light. "If this emerald is real, I bet it's worth some serious dough."

"It's a fancy rare green diamond, not an emerald," Ruby corrected him. "And yes, it was stolen from me. From my house when Suki was killed," Ruby defended Sydney.

"How do you know it's the same green diamond?" Officer Mellon asked.

"Well, how many fancy green diamonds from Africa of this size would be floating around the city? Or around the state, for that matter?" Ruby asked.

"I'm not a gemologist, and the last time I checked neither is Detective Niver." The two detectives grinned at each other. "While you may have a good point, the first thing is to establish that this stone is the same one identified in the GIA study and in your aunt's will. If it is, then, we will need to question your former attorney. If it's not, then we will be making"—Detective Mellon looked directly at Sydney—"your arrest."

"We have something else we want to talk to you about." Officer Mellon spoke directly to Ruby now.

"You're excused." Officer Niver looked at Sydney as if she were a student leaving detention. "You can wait in the lobby. We won't be too much longer." He opened the door and watched her walk out.

"Suki's boyfriend, Armando Lewis, has checked out." Niver nodded his head like a bobble head doll, smirking to one side of his mouth, revealing a single dimple in his unshaven cheek.

"What do you mean, checked out?" Ruby asked.

"Meaning," Niver continued, "he had an alibi. He's back in the county jail on a weapons charge. Been in for a couple of weeks." He waited for Ruby to respond.

She said nothing, waiting for him to continue.

"We did find two different fingerprints in the house besides Suki's—yours and one we couldn't identify. So, who were you with that night?"

Chapter 20

The next morning, the news got wind that Suki's criminal ex-boyfriend had been exonerated while her roommate—a daytime butterfly keeper and former nightclub singer-turned-heiress with no record—and a horse trainer with a questionable record were the focus of the investigation. The news spread like wildfire. While they were not named "suspects" formally, Ruby Sans and Owen Kierney were now considered "persons of interest." Neither had been arrested nor charged with any crime.

Ruby wanted to call Suki's mom to explain the situation but didn't know how to get in touch with her. She hadn't gotten her number when she spoke with her on the phone at the Green Gable Estate. Ruby knew Suki's mother would be expecting her attendance at Suki's memorial, but given the recent news story, Ruby wasn't sure attending was such a good idea. She was concerned about the message it would send if she didn't show up, but it could be a lot worse if she did. She didn't want to answer questions about how she found Suki; and deep down, she held herself responsible for Suki's death because she was convinced that Suki was murdered over the diamond.

Ruby decided to hold her own memorial service to honor Suki in a more personal way instead, and then go to the Conservatory to work for a while afterwards. Although she planned to cut down her hours, she was committed to seeing her current project through to completion, which was creating a huge butterfly display in the entry hall of the museum.

Sometimes, on Ruby's lunch break, Suki would meet her at "their spot" on the river just a few minutes' walking distance from the museum. On the north side of the pedestrian bridge there was a cement stage—a small amphitheater of sorts where weddings and one-act plays were performed in the summers. Behind the amphitheater there was a space just large enough for two or three people, depending on their size, to sit on the cement ledge above the river. If the water wasn't up too high, you could dangle your legs over without touching the swift-moving current.

Ruby and Suki had been there at least a dozen times. The last time, Suki had stopped at the 7-Eleven first to get a pint of mint chocolate chip ice cream for them to share and two plastic spoons. They sat together, taking turns spooning the green minty coldness, discussing how fortunate Suki was to finally be free of Armando; how she could start her life again; that she was worthy and capable of happiness. Despite her periodic lapses in judgment, Suki was an exuberant soul who loved with her entire being.

With a small brown paper bag in hand, Ruby climbed carefully up onto the backside of the amphitheater. The water was up higher than usual, so she had to sit cross-legged on the cement so as not to get drenched or swept away. As a matter of ceremony, from the bag, she pulled out a pint of mint ice cream and two plastic spoons. She pressed the bag down flat on the cement beside her and set the spoons on it. She opened the lid of the ice cream carton and pulled back the plastic lining. With one of the spoons, she scooped out a spoonful of the green, creamy goodness and let it melt on her tongue. She left the other, Suki's spoon, on the bag.

In the distance, she noticed two people—a man and a woman in a red coat standing on the footbridge. One of the reasons Ruby and Suki had loved "their spot" so much was that they could watch people coming and going across the footbridge without anyone seeing them. The tree limbs on the side of the amphitheater cement ledge obstructed the view if you were standing on the bridge. They even tested it out one time.

Not wanting any more of the ice cream, Ruby set her spoon alongside Suki's. With both hands, she reached behind her neck and unclasped her half-heart "friends" necklace. She held it in her palms as the water ran southward beneath. Her tears dropped onto the silver. She wondered if she would ever know who'd murdered her best friend. Although she couldn't explain how Morgan had the diamond, she had a hard time believing that he would kill Suki. The only time he saw Suki—to Ruby's knowledge— was when Suki waved out the window the day he picked up Ruby at the house. Any connection between Morgan and Suki didn't make sense.

Ruby took the necklace and held it at the clasp, allowing the chain and half pendant to hang. She said a prayer in silence and then let go of the necklace, watching it as it dropped into the water below. That was when she heard the woman scream.

* * *

Ruby turned to look in the direction of the footbridge. The man and woman seemed to be struggling, but it was hard to tell. Ruby remembered she had a small pair of binoculars in her purse that she'd bought for GP's upcoming race. She quickly pulled them out and turned them inward to focus. It took a moment for her eyes to adjust. She could see the woman in her red poodle wool coat leaning over the railing, but she couldn't tell if the man was pushing the woman or trying to pull her back. Ruby needed to further adjust the focus.

The woman screamed a second time. It took Ruby a moment to readjust the focus and find the couple in her view again. Her hands were a bit shaky. She saw that the man was holding the woman now safely on the footing of the bridge and patting her on the back. The woman had her head buried in his chest. The man turned his head. Ruby sharpened the focus to see if she could see it more clearly. The man on the bridge was Julian Kleptstein!

Ruby kept her focus on the couple, waiting for the woman to turn her head so she could get a clear view of her face as well. If Ruby were only a little higher, she could probably make it out. She grabbed the branch of one of the trees with one hand for support while she held the binoculars in the other. She pulled herself up into a standing position, careful not to kick the ice cream, the bag, or the spoons into the water below. She looked through the binoculars again, but it was too late. The couple had turned away and crossed the bridge. Ruby's foot slipped off the ledge and her other hand instinctively grabbed the tree branch, sending the binoculars into the river below.

Chapter 21

"There's a bench on the other side of the bridge." Kleptstein led Kursta by the hand across the bridge and down a walking path to a molded cement bench displaying a bronze plaque dedicated to someone he didn't know. He sat her down.

She was shaking and sobbing.

"Listen to me." He put his hands squarely on her shoulders. "Look at me." Kursta slowly raised her gaze to meet Kleptstein's.

"You need to get ahold of yourself. You need to talk about it. You asked me here. Here I am. You need to tell me what's going on, Kursta. Are you in some kind of trouble?"

She didn't answer him at first. She pressed her lips together firmly and tears streamed down her face. Finally, she whispered, "I'm worried for Owen."

Kleptstein pulled back from her with his arms still holding her shoulders so he could study her face. "Owen, your son?"

"He's been linked to that bartender's murder."

"Do you think he had anything to do with it?"

Kursta stared at him and said nothing.

Kleptstein couldn't tell if her look was of disbelief or fear.

"Owen is a good man, Klept. He is." It was as if Kursta was trying to convince herself.

Kleptstein nodded.

"I hope he wasn't involved." Kursta started breathing

rapidly.

"You hope? You think there is a chance?"

"Please, don't share this with anyone. I mean, I'm getting close to you." Tears started welling in her eyes. "Do you feel it, too, Klept?"

He smiled at her compassionately. "Feel what?"

"Is it just me? I want to let you in. I want to trust you." Kursta was waiting for him to respond.

"You can tell me anything." He smiled. Kleptstein knew he was in trouble. Kursta was speaking so cryptically. He wasn't sure if Kursta was trying to tell him that Owen had killed Suki or that she was falling for him. Suddenly, Ruby's face flashed in his head. If he could just listen to what Kursta had to say—to play along at least—maybe she would say something that would prove Ruby's innocence in the process.

Kursta turned to look back down at the river. Kleptstein kept both hands on her shoulders and fixed his gaze on her face. "There's something you're not telling me."

Kursta turned back to look at him. "I'm in fear of my life."

Chapter 22

Ruby had just finished mounting a Junonia Coenia, or Common Buckeye, on a four-inch square board in the butterfly lab when the phone rang. The Buckeye was one of Ruby's favorite butterfly species for its subtle beauty. While not as striking from a distance as a Swallowtail or a Monarch, up close the vibrant blue and purple eyes lined in black were nothing short of hypnotizing. This poor beauty Ruby worked on had ended its lifecycle under one of the Conservatory bushes. Most of the butterflies in the new display would be repurposed from the butterfly habitat. They would be mounted as if the wind had kicked them up and sent them flying in a scrolling looping formation; something they would never do in their natural lives, but together they would make an incredible eye-catching display to greet the guests as they entered the building.

The phone rang again. Ruby picked it up and held the phone between her ear and her shoulder as she eyeballed her work to make sure it was straight. "This is Ruby," she answered.

"Yes, Ruby, this is Mil Morgan. I'm sorry to bother you at work, but there's something I need to inform you."

"What's that?" she sighed and stepped away from the lab table.

"Given your current status in the Suki Giles investigation, I am relinquishing myself as your estate attorney."

"OK. Is there anything else you wanted to tell me?"

She shifted her weight on to her other foot and crossed her arms.

"You will need to hire a defense attorney."

Ruby waited for him to continue. There was a long pause. "Is that it?" She asked. "Is that all?"

"That is all." Morgan hung up the phone.

Ruby put the phone handset on the cradle. She didn't believe that was all he had to say.

Now that her aunt's estate was settled, Ruby could see no reason to have further contact with Morgan. She didn't trust him, and she didn't believe he'd served her aunt well at all. Rather, she believed that Morgan had taken advantage of Hilde; and for all she knew, Kursta and Owen may have done so as well. She was convinced Kursta and Owen's horse business with her aunt was all a convenient set-up of Morgan's contriving. If it weren't for Morgan, Ruby would not be inappropriately linked to the death of her best friend, and Suki may still be alive.

* * *

Ruby bristled at statements made by the media alleging she and Owen were in a relationship. Some stories talked about their hot, steamy night together that got a little rough, causing the bump on her head.

Sydney called Ruby when the latest story hit the local TV station. "The news isn't being very kind to you, my friend. I have some information on your criminal wingman you should know about. I'll tell you in the car on the way to the race."

The cloud of the investigation hung over Ruby as she prepared to attend her first horse race. She had purchased a fancy peacock-blue dress with a matching blue-and-black fascinator with two peacock feathers poking out one side to wear, but ended up wearing a tamed-down navy version without the feathers. She thought it would be better not to draw so much attention to herself. Sydney completely foiled the plan by wearing a hot pink polka-dotted dress and a matching broad-brimmed pink straw hat with a huge pink polka-dotted bow facing the back. If Ruby stood next to Sydney at the race, there was attention to be drawn.

"So, do tell all you know about Owen Kierney. I feel like you have been holding out on me." Ruby scowled as they moved with the flow of traffic in Sydney's navy-blue Volkswagen Jetta to the race.

"I didn't know he took you to the Bash that night. He's quite magnetic, isn't he?" Sydney looked over and smiled at Ruby, almost hitting her in the face with her hat in the process.

"I thought you actually had something important to tell me about him."

"Oh, I have plenty to tell you. I was just curious what you thought of him."

"I don't know the point of all this, but no. I mean, I'll admit I was attracted to him that night at dinner. Then once we got to the Bash, he left me alone for quite some time and then didn't even take me to the hospital after I fell and hit my head. I could have had a concussion or worse. Then, the next morning, he accused me of being a black out drunk. Honestly, Syd, I'm not sure I didn't sleep with him that night. I really don't remember much about the entire evening except a conversation I had with a mysterious Asian woman at the Bash who told me to watch out for Owen and his mother. She also said GamePlan was not favored to win, regardless of what Owen told me."

"Well, no judgment here." Sydney kept her eyes on the road.

"Sydney, I felt like I had been drugged that night. I think someone slipped a hallucinogenic into my drink."

"Ah yes, the Evening Initiator."

"You know about it?"

"Yes, but the rumors were never confirmed." Sydney looked over her shoulder and changed lanes, hitting Ruby on the side of the face with her hat in the process.

"Ouch," Ruby winced. "Seriously, Sydney, I believe I was drugged that night."

"Well, who would you report it to? The police? Do you think it would make a difference now that you are a person of interest?"

Sydney did have a point.

"Since we are on the topic of rumors, do you remember when I told you about Kursta being linked to some possible racehorse deaths?"

"Yes," Ruby answered. "Keep looking straight ahead or you'll hit me in the face again."

Sydney tried to keep her eyes on the road. "Well, Owen was the main suspect. His famous Kentucky training regimen was blamed for killing horses. Oddly enough, only the ones that weren't performing up to par or were suddenly injured with no siring potential were dying. The most famous case was the one of a big dark bay called Kingston."

"He told me about that horse. My aunt was supposedly the co-owner with Kursta."

"Did he tell you how he died?"

"Yes, he collapsed after a race."

"There was a story written about Owen. It was called 'Dark Horse.' They never had enough evidence to arrest him or his mother."

Sydney pulled into the owners' parking lot. As soon as they parked, a young reporter appeared at Ruby's side of the car.

The woman pushed her big fat microphone into Ruby's face as she tried to exit the vehicle. "Ms. Sans, can I please get a statement from you about your roommate? Did you kill Suki Giles?"

"No, of course I didn't." Ruby tried to remain calm as she walked toward the stands.

"Have you seen Owen Kierney today? Will you be watching the race with him?" the reporter asked.

"No, I'm here with my friend."

"Is Owen Kierney no longer a friend of yours?"

Ruby decided to refrain from giving the reporter any other information that she could use to formulate another question.

"Did you and Owen kill Suki together? Was it some sort of love triangle?"

Ruby started to come unraveled inside. "No further comments." She walked with long strides while Sydney struggled to keep up with her.

Ruby headed straight for the wager booth, where she picked up a program and a racing card to place her bet.

The stands were full. Ruby and Sydney settled into their box seat. Ruby remembered her binoculars were at the bottom of the river. Thankfully, Sydney brought a pair.

Ruby looked at the Tote Board. "We still have twenty minutes before the race starts. An eternity."

Ruby felt someone tap her on the shoulder. She turned to see it was Julian Kleptstein. A chill raised on her arm. She remembered seeing him that day on the bridge when she lost her binoculars. She wished she could ask him who the woman was that almost went over the railing. And even stranger, she recalled the incident at the Green Gable Estate, when she thought she saw him and then found the rose on the doorstep.

"Oh my goodness! How are you?" She smiled, holding back a flood of thoughts.

"You look beautiful as ever, Ruby." Kleptstein looked at her from head to toe and then back up again.

Ruby felt like the man was drinking in her soul. She felt queasy.

"Are you still singing?"

She felt a thud in her chest. "I haven't lately. You may have heard—"

He interrupted her. "Ruby, you have a lovely voice and the world needs to hear it. I need to hear it."

His words made her feel like she had dozens of ants

crawling all over her body. She shivered.

"Are you cold?" he asked, placing a hand on her shoulder briefly. "I understand you are no longer singing at Curiocity. Are you going to be singing at another club?"

"I'm not sure yet. I have a lot going on right now, as I'm sure you've heard."

"I'm so sorry to hear about your roommate."

"Thank you." Ruby couldn't wait for the interaction to end. She glanced over to Sydney, who seemed keenly interested in their conversation.

"Ruby, I know you did not kill Suki Giles."

Ruby bit her lip and nodded her head.

"You know she gave me your phone number, don't you?"

Ruby nodded again. She didn't understand the point of his question. While the conversation grew stranger by the moment, a voice inside her told her to see beyond the man's peculiarity and to listen to what he had to say. Perhaps he knew who killed Suki or had some kind of clue.

"Suki was your best friend." Kleptstein's words came out slow and deliberate. "You wouldn't kill your best friend."

"No, I wouldn't." Ruby was searching for the punch line. His comments seemed to be isolated statements, unconnected to any specific point. Was he just making up conversation as an excuse to be close to her? She figured she shouldn't have to endure much longer; the race would be starting soon.

"There's something I need to tell you privately." Kleptstein motioned for her to step outside the box for a moment. Ruby wondered what he could possibly have to say to her now. She could almost hear Suki's voice in her head. *Beware of the creepy rose guy, Tuesday.*

Ruby glanced at Sydney briefly and smiled in nervousness as she stepped out into the aisle. She pinched the underside of her arm as Kleptstein leaned over to whisper in her ear, his nose just under her earlobe. She thought she heard him take in a brief inhale as if he were drawing in her scent. She dug her nails in deeper. Chills rose all over her body.

"I know who has your diamond," he whispered.

The bugler signaled the race would start in ten minutes. Ruby looked at Kleptstein with wide eyes.

He handed her his business card. "Call me and I'll tell you more." He smiled. "I hope your horse does well today." He turned away and was off to find his place in the crowd.

Ruby stepped back into the box beside Sydney, who was now standing with the rest of the onlookers in anticipation of the start of the race.

"You'll have to tell me all about that weirdo after the race." Sydney put her binoculars up to her face.

The jockeys led their horses to the gate in order: 1. John's Lime Twig; 2. Patterson; 3. Chimera; 4. GamePlan; and 5. Flannery. Buckeyes formed in the pit of Ruby's gut and she finally understood the draw of the electric track—like a blue light attracting moths.

Roman Drewster wore colors that Kursta had allowed Hilde to choose when she bought her share of GP: royal blue, bright green, and canary yellow. Ruby noticed that GP was a bit antsy and Roman had some difficulty getting him to walk in a straight line to the gate. Flannery was also a bit jumpy. The horses entered their stalls.

Sydney handed her binoculars to Ruby. "Here, use these."

The gates opened. "And they're off!" the announcer called.

The horses exited their stalls together, and at first it appeared some would collide. Flannery bobbled for a moment but regained his composure and fell in line behind GamePlan, who was in third position. GP drafted John's Lime Twig in second on the inside as Chimera held the lead. Patterson was in fifth, then moved into fourth as he slipped between Flannery and GP.

The entire crowd stood. The horses rounded the first

corner. GP was edging closer to John's Lime Twig.

"He's gaining! He's gaining!" Ruby tingled with excitement. She pulled the binoculars away for a moment to take in the whole of the track, the sounds of the crowd around her, and the smell of the air. She then resumed her view through the binoculars.

The horses were on the back stretch. Dirt was flying. Ruby heard someone behind her say that the track was fast. GamePlan was now in second position behind Chimera as John's Lime Twig fell back to third. GP gained a bit so that he and Chimera vied for first position. Patterson gained on the outside. Chimera also moved ahead but dangerously close to GP. GP became wedged between Chimera and Patterson. John's Lime Twig then gained on the outside, trapping GP.

"GamePlan is caught in a blind switch," the announcer called.

Ruby bit her lip. "What does that mean?" She handed the binoculars to Sydney.

"It's when a horse gets trapped between or behind the others. Sometimes the only way out of it is to pull the horse back." Sydney looked through the lens.

"There won't be enough time," Ruby surmised.

The horses rounded the final corner. Ruby could hear the pounding of the horses' hooves coming closer. "And here they come into the final stretch!" the announcer called, and the crowd went wild. It looked as if Roman might try to pull GP back to get out of the trap, but suddenly Chimera pulled ahead of GP and Patterson, creating just enough room for GP to pull out of the pocket. Roman pulled out all the stops with GP, using the switch. GP started gaining again. He passed Patterson, pushing harder and harder, but there wasn't enough track. GP came in second behind Chimera.

Seconds later, Chimera was announced the winner.

Ruby's heart sank. Sydney gave her a consolatory hug. "I'm really surprised Roman got caught in that blind switch. Usually seasoned jockeys can outmaneuver them."

"I want to go see GP." Ruby stuck out her bottom lip.

"Are you sure that's such a good idea?" Sydney asked. "The reporters will have a field day with you and Owen being so close in proximity."

"The media will do what the media will do. I'm not going to let them stand in the way of me seeing my horse."

Ruby made her way through the crowd with Sydney following behind.

"So, she did show up," Roman Drewster announced still atop GamePlan. Owen Kierney stood next to the horse and watched as Ruby and Sydney approached. He was visibly agitated when he recognized them.

"Oh no, no, no, no, no," Owen said walking up to them. Ruby thought he was talking to her, but he bypassed her to get to Sydney. He stood close to her, looking down and pointing his long, tan finger in her face as if he were reprimanding a child.

"You don't need to be here. I don't need any reporters writing a bunch of shit about me." He turned to Ruby. "Is she one of your friends?"

Ruby looked at the two of them in complete confusion. "What's going on here?"

"This woman almost ruined my entire career." Owen was still pointing his finger in Sydney's face. "Have you read the article she wrote about me? It's called 'Dark Horse.'"

Ruby turned to Sydney. "You didn't tell me you wrote the article. You're a reporter? I thought you were a Legal Secretary."

Other people had gathered around. Kursta was there, and Kleptstein was with her! The situation was getting more surreal by the moment. Ruby wondered if the woman on the bridge that day was Kursta. Were the "Hometown Heroes" an item? What about Morgan? He was nowhere to be found, thank goodness.

"I'll explain on the ride home," Sydney said to Ruby.

"I'll just excuse myself and stand over here to the side. Let me know when you're ready to go."

Owen walked over to Ruby. "You should know who you're associating with, Ms. Sans."

"I couldn't agree more." She turned her attention to Roman Drewster and GamePlan.

"Dreeki's a shyster. We should've won. Kursta, you have got to do something with Dreeki. He plays dirty." Spiro Dreeki was Chimera's jockey. "You saw what he did. He purposely pushed his horse into GP. You know what that's called? It's called Careless Riding. Look it up, rule number sixteen ninety-nine. There was no way Chimera could have pulled ahead if it weren't for Dreeki pulling that dirty move. Not to mention, he could have injured both horses. There's no excuse for that kind of behavior, and owners" —Roman looked directly at Ruby—"shouldn't stand for that, you know?"

Ruby couldn't understand half of what Roman was saying. If he was expecting her to do something, she had no idea what that was.

Kursta spoke up. "We will be discussing it at the next association meeting, but honestly Roman, you should have been able to get out of it."

"And I did get out of it, just not soon enough. You know it's bullshit, Kursta. You know it! He should get three racing days' penalty for that. It's called 'failure to make a proper effort to maintain a straight course in the stretch and causing interference.' Do you even know the Rule Book?" Roman reined GP around like he was headed for the paddock. He stopped and turned back around. "Now that I'm on a roll, I might as well tell you that I called the Racing Board myself this morning. I am not going to stand for one more perfectly healthy horse dying around here from 'natural causes.'" He put his hands up in quotation marks. "You certainly aren't doing anything about it!" Roman looked directly at Kursta.

Owen pulled Ruby aside. "I need to talk to you," he

said in a low tone.

"What did Roman mean by that?" Ruby's eyes darted around to see if anyone was listening.

"Another horse was found dead in its stable this morning after it raced yesterday."

"What do you mean, another horse?"

"A horse was found dead a few weeks ago in the paddock the morning after its last race. They never found out the cause of death. There was another one today. They both died the morning after their races."

"That's very suspicious." Ruby grew uncomfortable and looked around. "We shouldn't draw attention to each other. We are just going to fuel the media. They already accosted me on my way in to the track."

"They caught me on the backside, too." The edge in his voice softened. "I have some guys looking out for them. They're gone now. Just keep your little legal secretary friend in check. Do you even know about her?"

Ruby admitted to herself that she didn't know much about this woman who seemed to have an interesting sense of right and wrong, and had befriended her pretty rapidly.

Owen put his hand on the front of Ruby's shoulder. "I am so sorry about what happened the night of the Bash. I didn't use my best judgment and I realize now that I should have taken you to the hospital."

Ruby's inner critic quieted for the moment.

"And I am so sorry about your friend. I feel terrible that you had to go into the house by yourself and find her like that. I can't stop thinking about what might have happened if I had taken you home that night."

"Maybe she wouldn't be dead."

"Or maybe you both would be."

"Have you spoken to the police?" Ruby looked up into his bottomless green eyes.

"Yes, once. I thought you knew that. Listen, now is not the time to talk about this. Will you meet me somewhere?"

Owen pleaded.

Ruby could feel Kleptstein's gaze upon her. She looked in his direction and he locked eyes with her. She turned her body slightly so he could not read her lips. "Meet me at the Hotel Meridien lobby at two p.m. tomorrow."

Chapter 23

"So when were you planning to tell me that you wrote the story, 'Dark Horse'?" Ruby pressed Sydney in the car on the ride home. "And since when have you been a reporter?" she asked in a highly irritated tone.

"I've been an amateur journalist since college. I freelance. I was going to tell you I wrote the article. I just needed to know about your relationship with Owen Kierney first. Had you thought he was a good guy or were falling for him, I knew you wouldn't believe what I had to say."

Ruby couldn't argue with that.

"As a matter of fact, when I interviewed him for the story, I thought I might bag it entirely. Everything he had to say was terribly convincing. He was able to explain away the death of Kingston and two other horses under his charge. I must admit, I scheduled a couple of follow up interviews before running the story just so I could see him."

"So, you were smitten with him, too. Why did you run the story?"

"Because the evidence against him was still compelling. Sure, not enough to convict him; but all three horses' tox screens came back positive for a supplement that in high doses could lead to death."

"That doesn't mean he did it." Ruby admitted to herself that she was defending him.

"True, but all three horses died while under his care."

The end of their conversation was perfectly timed with Sydney pulling up to the entrance of the hotel.

"When are you going to move into your aunt's estate?" Sydney asked as Ruby started to get out of the car.

"I guess as soon as I'm ruled out as a suspect in Suki's murder." Ruby wasn't looking forward to going up to her room alone. "Do you want to come in for a coffee or a glass of wine?" Ruby asked Sydney.

"Sure, I'll drop you off here and park the car. I'll be there in a minute."

Ruby was relieved to have company a bit longer. She walked up to the hotel counter.

"You have a message," a young man said, handing Ruby an embossed envelope. It was the hotel's stationery. She opened it up as she proceeded to the café.

Ruby, please call Detective Niver. 555-8953.

She put the note back in its envelope and slipped it into her purse.

Sydney met Ruby at the café counter where they ordered their drinks.

Just as they sat down at a small table in the corner of the café lobby, Ruby spotted two uniformed police officers walk in.

"Cops." Ruby said it an on observation, not a warning. Sydney glanced up momentarily from the paper she had picked up from the counter. They seemed to know exactly where they were going, and they were headed in Ruby and Sydney's direction.

"Are they coming over here?" Sydney asked, not lifting her eyes from the paper this time.

"Yep," Ruby said, a bad feeling coming over her.

"Do you think it's about the diamond?" Sydney swallowed hard.

The officers loomed over them now. "Are you Sydney Tracey?" The dark Hispanic man with a buzz cut, wearing a dark-blue uniform stepped to stand directly over Sydney.

"Yes." She folded the paper into her lap and looked up

to make eye contact with the policeman.

The other officer, a stocky redhead with an overly pink face stood silent.

"We need to have a word with you."

Sydney seemed worried now and set the paper down on the marble bistro table separating her and Ruby.

"What's this about?" Ruby asked, knowing it was a bad idea.

"Ms. Sans," the talking officer looked at her, "Thank you for your concern, but this is something that doesn't involve you."

Ruby wondered if the town's entire police force knew her name.

"Ms. Tracey, would you please step over here with us?" The officer didn't specify where "here" was.

Sydney stood up and was clearly uncomfortable. Her face and neck were a blotchy red. The officer stepped about ten feet away from the table. Sydney and the other officer followed him.

Ruby strained to hear what the officer was saying to Sydney, but she couldn't make it out. The room seemed to go silent and everyone's sideways glances showed their attention on the two officers and the young blond woman.

The officer said something that made Sydney tear up and then he handcuffed her. Sydney turned her head to look at Ruby in a wide-eyed gaze. Ruby stood up to approach the officers. The redheaded one looked at her and put his hand out in a gesture that he acknowledged she'd better not step closer.

The officers led Sydney out of the building. The redhead wrapped his large fingers around Sydney's thin triceps, as if she might pose some kind of threat. Really?

Ruby remembered what Kleptstein had said at the race—that he knew who had her diamond. She pulled out his business card and walked quickly to the house phone in the lobby to make a call.

"Clobert's." It was a man's voice.

"May I speak with Mr. Kleptstein?"

"This is he."

"It's Ruby Sans. I'm glad I caught you." She couldn't believe those words had actually come out of her mouth given her encounter with him just a couple of hours before. "I wasn't sure you'd be at your shop so soon after the race."

"I'm sorry your horse didn't win today."

Ruby shuddered briefly. "Thanks. Listen, I need to see you right away. Do you mind if I meet you there at your shop?"

"No, by all means, do come by. We are under construction right now with the building of the new gemology institute, so just follow the signs to the entrance." He lingered for a beat. "I'm looking forward to seeing you, Ruby."

Ruby quivered, hanging up the phone. She exited the hotel just in time to see the police car pull away from the parking lot with Sydney in the back. Her heart sounded an alarm in her ears. She walked as fast as she could to the street corner and pushed the crosswalk button repeatedly until the light turned green.

Ruby made her way through the maze of plywood and blue tarp before she found the glass door with the sign that read, *Open During Construction*. Bells on the door announced her arrival. Three showroom clerks in business attire were eager to greet her, as if she had been their only customer that day. She was relieved that she would not be in the building alone with Kleptstein.

"Can I help you?" a man of about thirty with a perfectly trimmed beard, mindlessly twirling his pinky ring asked behind one of the glass jewelry counters.

"I have an appointment with Mr. Kleptstein." Ruby stated, wondering if his work associates called him "Klept," as he was known around Curiocity.

"I can see if he is in for you. What is your name?" the man asked.

"Ruby Sans."

"And, did you have something to pick up?"

"No, he'll know who I am."

A few moments later, Kleptstein rolled out with a beaming smile and a big creepy hug for Ruby, with a kiss on both cheeks; just an excuse to kiss her, no doubt. He showed her to the back of the building, to his private office. Ruby could hear the workers whispering as she passed them.

"I wasn't sure you would get in touch with me." Kleptstein locked eyes with Ruby. "It's so good to see you again. Are you doing all right?"

That was a loaded question, which Ruby could have answered in so many ways, but she decided to get to the point. "I'm fine but I want to know what you wanted to talk to me about at the race. You said you knew who had my diamond... or diamonds. What did you mean by that?" Ruby met his gaze.

"Mr. Morgan, who I assume is your attorney—"

"Was my attorney..." Ruby corrected him.

"And your aunt's attorney, right?"

After a moment, Ruby nodded her head.

"Mr. Morgan brought in two diamonds to be appraised for a client. One was imprinted with an identification number and had an accompanying study done by the Gemological Institute of America—the GIA. It's a pretty well known diamond. It's called by many in the industry as the Finian Star." He stopped to look at her.

"Go on," Ruby pressed.

"The other looked very similar, identical, to the other—to the untrained eye, that is. However, it is worlds apart. It so closely resembles a famous blood diamond, the Green Canary, from a mine in Africa. I believe it actually is the Green Canary, but I wouldn't be able to tell for sure without a GIA study. Morgan didn't mention anything about it changing colors. I don't think he knew what he had in his possession."

"What do you mean, changing colors?"

"There is an extremely rare kind of diamond called a Chameleon. It changes colors under certain heating and lighting conditions; the term is thermochromism. The famous Green Canary is a fancy green diamond, much like the one in the GIA study; however, when it is subjected to heat—especially emitted from a light source—at about three hundred ninety-two degrees Fahrenheit, it turns a bright canary yellow. When it cools down, it reverts back to its natural color. The Green Canary is one of the most famous chameleon blood diamonds in the world. I can hardly believe I had the opportunity to see it, or one like it."

"Why did you call it a blood diamond?" Ruby tilted her chin. "What does that mean?"

"Blood diamonds are used in the black market for extortion. They can be worth millions of dollars and are used to trade for weapons, drugs, even people's lives. The Green Canary has been lost for years. It was originally discovered in a mine in Central Africa by an East Indian Geologist by the name of Amir Dhanuka in the 1950s. He bequeathed it to his son, Nuhr Dhanuka, who died mysteriously in the mine one night. It was assumed he was killed for the diamond. It is one of the most significant diamond finds in history. The jewel belongs in a museum for people to see and understand the ugly history behind these beautiful stones. It is of the caliber of the Crown Jewels in the Tower of London."

"Is the other diamond also a blood diamond?" Ruby asked.

"More than likely." Kleptstein sighed, nodding his head.

"My aunt's will only mentioned one diamond, the one in the GIA study. That was the one I believe Morgan gave to me. It was stolen the night Suki was killed. I had no idea there was another diamond. However..." Ruby wondered whether she should continue.

"Ruby, I know this is difficult for you." Ruby noticed that Kleptstein's eyes were filled with compassion. "You can trust me. I am a professional. I have an obligation to my profession, to my reputation, to the institute, and to you as a friend..."

Ruby would hardly call him a friend; but in that moment, she wanted to trust Kleptstein.

"You were saying...? However...?" he prompted her.

Ruby took a deep breath. "However, my... friend was just arrested for stealing a fancy green diamond that looked like the one stolen from my house."

"Your friend? The one at the track with you?"

Ruby nodded. "She was Morgan's secretary. She went to his house looking for him. He has a history of... having accidents at home. Anyway, she found the diamond in his house and thought it was the one that was stolen from my place. I mean, how many large fancy green diamonds are there floating around, especially in a town like Tolstoy?"

"Right." Kleptstein nodded, encouraging her to continue.

"So, she took it and we brought it to the police."

"And they arrested her?"

"Well, they told her at the station that if it was the one that matched the GIA study, they wouldn't. They would then question Morgan. But, if it didn't match, they would."

"So, she must have stolen the Canary," Kleptstein concluded.

"She didn't steal it! Well, technically, but—"

"It was already stolen," Kleptstein stated matter-of-factly. "If your aunt had it, she had a stolen diamond."

"OK, so I need your help," Ruby got to the point. "My friend is in jail over this diamond, which she took from Morgan's house, but only because she thought it belonged to me. Now that we have established that this diamond was stolen a long time ago, we need to go to the police and tell them so they'll release Sydney."

"You want me to go to the police with you?" Kleptstein

raised his eyebrows.

"Don't you have a reference book or something that you can show them that the diamond was stolen a long time ago?"

"Yes, but it's not going to prove anything. We won't know that the diamond is the Canary or not until it is positively identified by the GIA." He turned to his credenza where he pulled a reference book on diamond values, a very thick leather-bound book. "I'll make you a copy."

"Thank you. Why won't you go to the police with me?" Ruby asked.

"I've had enough interaction with the police over the mugging incident at the printers to last me a few decades. Plus, they don't do anything for me here. No protection. I've got millions of dollars' worth of diamonds in my store. I ask for extra patrols, I don't get anything from them."

"I'll pay you." Ruby blurted out.

"No, no." Kleptstein waved his hand and made a face as if he smelled something repugnant. "I am not taking your money." He paused for a moment and then put his hand to his chin in thought.

"OK, I'll go to the police with you on one condition. You agree to have dinner with me tonight."

Chapter 24

The police station was within walking distance—about fifteen minutes away. Ruby would not be caught in a vehicle with Kleptstein under any circumstances, and in the time it would take for her to walk back to the hotel to get her own car, she could already be at the station. With the reference volume under his arm and Ruby by his side, Kleptstein did not seem in any particular hurry to get to their destination.

Since Kleptstein was getting a date out of her, Ruby decided to pry some information out of him. She knew she would be pushing the envelope but took her chances.

"So, I saw you the other day." Ruby picked up her pace in attempt to get Kleptstein to speed up. It helped a little.

"Oh yeah? Where was that?"

"At the river. Actually, on the pedestrian bridge."

He turned to her. "And where were you?"

"On the riverbank below. It was before I went to work at the museum; you know, at the animal exploration park."

"Oh, so you work at the museum, too?"

Great. Now Kleptstein would be tracking her at work. They approached a crosswalk and Ruby pushed the button at the light.

"Mmm hmm. I noticed you weren't alone."

"You are awfully interested in me. I'm surprised." Kleptstein smiled widely.

Ruby continued to walk at a quick clip. The station was only a couple of blocks away now. "The woman you were with screamed."

"Yes, then you saw that she slipped and almost went over the railing."

"It's a pretty high railing."

"She was quite distraught. I pulled her down. Calmed her down."

They started walking again. There was a pause of silence between them. The police station was only a block away now.

"You act like you don't know who she is," Kleptstein continued.

"I couldn't tell."

"But you could tell who I was?"

It was probably best to end the conversation as they were now walking up the sidewalk to the entrance.

"So," Kleptstein laughed, "have you been stalking me?"

* * *

Once inside the police station, Ruby walked up to the counter. Kleptstein sat down in one of the chairs in the empty lobby.

"May I speak with Detective Niver?" Ruby asked the clerk at the window. "He left me a message to get in touch with him."

The clerk leaned back in her rolling desk chair and called to someone out of view, "Is Niver here?" She looked back at Ruby. "Detective Niver is not here."

"What about Detective Mellon?"

The clerk leaned back again. "Mellon?"

She looked back at Ruby. "Detective Mellon is not here either."

Two strikes. Ruby decided to ask about Sydney. "Can you tell me how long Sydney Tracey will be in custody?"

The woman looked at her. "You mean at the jail? You're in the wrong place. The jail is two blocks away."

"Will you please have Detective Niver or Mellon call

me as soon as possible?"

The woman handed her a clipboard with a tablet and a pen. "Write your name and number on this."

Ruby wrote down her contact information on the paper and handed it back to the woman.

"No dice?" Kleptstein asked, seeing that Ruby hadn't gotten very far with the clerk.

"No. The detectives aren't here. I guess I should have called first." Ruby resigned herself.

"Where would you like to go to dinner?" Kleptstein asked with a gleam in his eye.

Chapter 25

Ruby woke up from a dream crying. In the dream, she was in a classroom, crammed into a student desk built for a first-grader. Her legs didn't fit under the desk with her feet flat on the floor, so she had to stick them out straight-legged. The Asian lady from the Bash stood over her scolding, "I told you to do your homework!" She slapped Ruby on the wrist with a ruler. "You are smart enough to figure this out, but the question is, do you care?"

Ruby got dressed and walked over to the county library, which was only a few blocks away from the hotel. She asked for help finding periodical articles on racehorse deaths at Diamond Head Stables. The librarian, a small, mousy woman whose head had been buried in a novel, took her back to the microfiche section where she could look up newspapers from the last few years. She also showed her a section of the library where there were equine magazines.

Ruby found several articles on Kingston, including Sydney's "Dark Horse" story; two articles on the horse found dead nearly a month ago; as well as one written about the horse that had died that week. There were some interesting similarities in all three horses. They were all found in their stalls collapsed after a race; one was found the night of the race; the other two the following morning. They all had been racing very well for a period of time; and then after winning a major race, lost a series of races. They ranged in ages from four to six years. They were all in good health otherwise.

While the deaths were suspicious, there were no arrests or formal suspects.

Ruby then asked the librarian to help her find stories about GamePlan's race history.

"If you want to find the horse's racing statistics, not just articles written about the horse, you need to actually go to the track. They can give you the results for every race your horse has ever run." The librarian was very friendly, but as soon as she gave Ruby the information, she quickly dove back into her book—*Due for Discard*. How apropos.

Ruby drove to the racetrack and found the racing booth. A heavyset woman with a southern drawl told her she had to go to the commission office and pointed out the way.

"Ask for Anna Uchibori," the lady said. "I swear she is the smartest person I know. She will know all about your horse."

As Ruby climbed the stairs leading to the racing office, she hoped she wouldn't run into Kursta. She opened the door to the lobby. No one was there. There was a round metal push-button bell sitting on the counter. She pressed it a couple of times. She sat down and picked up an issue of *Blood-Horse* magazine.

"Oh, it's you." The Asian lady from the Bash walked in from the other room. "I was wondering when you were going to find me. I know you care about your horse, Miss Sans. You need to do something now so that he doesn't suffer the same fate as Kingston and the other two horses."

Ruby was mystified by this woman who infiltrated her dreams. "I did some research at the library this morning. I found similarities in the three horses that died, but I was told I needed to come here to get any stats on GP."

"That's good you do your homework. Did you see the pattern? They won a few races, even a major race, and then lost at least three races. The horses were not old. Not young in the racing world, but still not too old. You see that?" She looked at Ruby like the schoolteacher waiting for an answer from her student.

Ruby nodded her head. "Um, is Kursta around?"

The woman blinked hard several times, her brows going along for the ride. "No. Kursta is not here today. Lucky for you. Lucky for me, too." She smiled widely at Ruby. "Now, let's look at your horse." The woman went over to a bookshelf and stood on a stepladder so she could reach the top shelf. She pulled out a stats book labeled with GamePlan's name. She took it to the counter and opened it to show Ruby.

"We have books on every horse at Diamond Head. I have been looking in this one a lot lately. See here." She pointed to the middle of the page. "He won three races here at Diamond in the span of six months." She traced her finger to the next page. "Then, won a major race— the Santa Anita Derby. And then..." she turned the page "...a loss, another loss, and this week yet another loss. It was close, but still a loss." She looked at Ruby with that schoolteacher look again, waiting for her to say something.

Ruby just stared back at her.

"So, what do you think? Is your horse in a critical time?"

"A critical time?" Ruby repeated. "What are you saying? Didn't the horses die of natural causes?" Ruby asked.

"Hmmm... Sometimes it's hard to know why a horse dies. They are delicate animals; strong, but at the same time fragile. Like people." She blinked hard.

Ruby studied the woman's face, waiting for her to say more.

"Who owned the horses?" Ruby asked.

"They had multiple owners." The woman went back to the bookshelf and pulled the binders on the other three horses. She turned to the page in each binder showing the list of owners for each horse and set them all on the counter before Ruby.

Ruby looked at each one. Some horses had more

owners than others, understandably. "Kursta Blithey is listed as a co-owner on all these horses." Ruby saw the common thread.

"You're smart enough to figure this out. The question is, do you care?" The woman repeated the line from Ruby's dream.

"Are you saying that Kursta Blithey—your boss—killed these horses?"

"Never accuse anyone of anything until there is enough evidence. Better if you catch them in the act."

"Do you want to catch her in the act?" Ruby finally understood what the woman was really asking.

"Do you want to save your horse?" Anna asked.

Ruby nodded her head in seriousness, knowing there would likely be danger involved. Ruby looked down at her watch. It was 1:45 p.m. She realized she had to meet Owen at the hotel in fifteen minutes.

"I'm going to be late for an appointment with Owen Kierney."

"Kursta's son?" Anna asked.

"Yes." Ruby remembered Anna's warning about him at the Bash, and that she wasn't sure if he had actually charmed her pants off.

"I'm not so sure you can trust him. You be careful if you want to save your beautiful horse." Anna shook her head and blinked a couple of times. Ruby found Anna Uchibori to be very intimidating. "You come back tonight." Anna said it as an order.

"Tonight?" Ruby squinted her eyes and made a face.

"OK, look at race the schedule with me. Kursta is gone today and tonight. She's back tomorrow. Your horse races again in three days. You know the pattern."

"Well, what are we going to do?" Ruby asked.

"Just come back at nine o'clock tonight. You leave the planning to me. Oh, let me give you the code to the service gate since it will be locked when you come back."

Chapter 26

Ruby ran into the hotel out of breath. She looked around and spotted Owen sitting at the Hotel bar. She looked at her watch. Surprisingly, she was only ten minutes late; but she had hauled ass to get there.

"Why are you running, Girl?" He smiled when he saw her and took a swig of his bottle of Wild Horse amber ale. By the looks of him, Ruby figured that was not his first beer of the day. It was a little early to be drinking for her, but she figured she could make an exception.

"I'll have the same," she told the bartender. "You been here long? I'm sorry to keep you waiting." Ruby took a few deep breaths, trying to settle herself after her visit with Anna Uchibori.

"I wouldn't have guessed you to be a beer drinker."

"There are probably a lot of things you don't know about me, but don't worry, I'm not going to pass out—unless you slip something into my beer."

"Was that really necessary?" he sneered.

"I guess not."

The bartender handed Ruby her bottle and held up a glass in a silent question. She lifted the bottle and shook her head no in response to the bartender. Owen clinked her bottle with his bottle.

"Here's to new beginnings."

"I can drink to that," Ruby took a sip of her beer.

"So, tell me what you told the police." Ruby got down to business.

"I told them what happened; that we went to dinner at Dim Sum and then to the Racing Association party. You weren't feeling well so I took you back to my place. The next morning, I took you home. When I heard what happened on the news, I tried calling you multiple times, but of course you weren't home. I didn't know how to get a hold of you. You must have twenty messages on your answering machine at home. I have your dress in my car, by the way. Just got it back from the cleaners."

"Thank you." Ruby didn't want to get off topic. "Did you tell them that I hit my head?"

"No."

"They took pictures of me when they came to the house. Of my head."

"Well, I don't see the connection to your friend's murder. And for that matter, I am certain I wouldn't be considered a person of interest had we not spent the night together."

"Yeah, about that." Ruby started to pick at the label of her beer.

"Yeah, what about it?" He smiled. Before she could say anything, Owen blurted, "Nothing happened. I know you don't know me, but I would never take advantage of you, or anyone. Did you notice you were on the couch and not in my bed? Even if you were in my bed, it wouldn't matter."

Ruby wanted to trust him but kept hearing Anna's voice in her head.

"You're an attractive woman, I'm not going to lie; but believe it or not, and I realize you wouldn't come to this conclusion given our first date..."

Date? *Is that what he thought it was?* Ruby asked herself.

"...I am a decent human being. I may not always have the best judgment, as that night revealed, but I'm a good guy."

Oh, how she wanted to believe him. His green eyes

were drawing her in.

"I will do the right thing even when it's difficult." His eyeballs were getting very shiny and he bit his bottom lip.

"What are you talking about?" The Buckeyes took flight in her stomach.

"I have a confession to make."

Ruby held her breath in anticipation of what he would say next.

"I wasn't sure what to do with you that night at the Bash when you passed out and hit your head. I was freaking out. I poured you into the front seat of the Land Rover and went to your house. I was super embarrassed to take you home in that condition. I didn't know what your roommate would think of me. I didn't know how the whole thing might affect your relationship with her, but I told myself I would just tell her the truth and see if she could help me get you into the house and I'd stay up and watch over you to make sure you were OK. That was my plan."

Ruby sensed his sincerity. Her heart was pounding in anticipation of what she would hear next. "So how did it fall apart?"

"When we got to your house, there was a two-ton black Ford truck parked in front. A muscle truck. A guy's kind of truck. So, I thought Suki had company. Then, for sure, I was not going to take you into the house and interrupt something. I decided to just take you to my place where I could watch you and make sure you were OK."

"When I dropped you off at home the next morning, the truck wasn't there. I didn't say anything to you about it because that wasn't any of my business. What if your roommate didn't want you to know she had a guy over while you were gone? At the time, I figured that was between the two of you."

Ruby was silent. She felt sick to her stomach but wanted to know more.

"When the news hit the next morning that your

roommate was killed, then it became my business. I called you numerous times and didn't get any answer, but of course I called your house and it was a crime scene. I wanted to tell you that I had gone to the police. Just as soon as I heard the news, I went down to the station and told them I had seen the truck that night."

Ruby didn't know what to make of what Owen was telling her. "Did you get the license plate number?"

"No, why would I write down the license plate number of who I thought was Suki's boyfriend?"

He did have a point. Ruby was grasping for any clues that might lead to Suki's killer. "Suki didn't know anyone with a black Ford truck, and she certainly wasn't dating anyone. She was almost killed by her last boyfriend, and the police cleared him early on in the investigation. He was back in jail on a weapons charge. Probably still is."

"The detectives did ask me something strange, though."

"What's that?" She drained her beer.

"They asked me if I knew anything about a diamond being stolen from the house. Not any diamond, but some fancy one that looked like an emerald."

"Do you know anything about it?" Ruby was extremely curious to know what he would say next.

"No, do you? Supposedly it was in your house."

"Yes, I inherited it from Hilde. Morgan had just given it to me. It was stolen around the time Suki was killed. Almost the entire house was ransacked so I believe the killer was looking for the diamond."

"Your aunt was one wealthy lady. I suppose that makes you one now. You need to be careful." Owen took the last swallow of his beer.

"I see that." Ruby changed the subject. "What do you make of those two horses collapsing this month?"

"It's not good for Diamond Head, that's for sure. The Horse Racing Board is conducting an investigation."

"I understand your mother was partial owner of each

one of those horses. With Kingston's death, that makes three."

"And your point is?"

"She's the co-owner of GamePlan, my horse. GamePlan has a similar history to those other two horses that died this month. And to Kingston. And to two horses before him. You were those horses' trainer."

"I was the trainer of Kingston, and two horses in Kentucky; that is true. I am not—was not—the trainer of the two horses that died this month." Owen's tone became insistent. "I don't know what your little reporter friend told you, but I am not responsible for any racehorse deaths. The horses featured in her article were given a supplement that can show up on a tox screen, but what she failed to inform you was that they were not at toxic levels. I could test any racehorse right now for those supplements and ninety-nine percent would come out positive. GP is also on the same supplements."

"All of these horses have a similar race history, and GP's race history falls right in line with them. They win a few races, even a major race, only to be on a losing streak for a while."

"GamePlan was a contender in this last race. It was Drewster who screwed up. GP still has a lot of race left in him."

"He has a race in three days. Please make sure it is not his last."

Chapter 27

Ruby knocked on the racing association door at 9 p.m. sharp. She saw through the glass door that the lobby was dark but there was a light on in the back office.

A large man with long dirty blond hair opened the door in the dark. He didn't turn the light on. He didn't say anything. Something told Ruby not to ask for Anna. She had to make something up quick.

"I'm here to drop off my membership dues," Ruby told the man, who didn't seem happy she was there.

"At nine o'clock at night? How did you get through the gate?"

"I have a code. I'm an owner."

"Didn't you know this office closed at five p.m.?"

"No, I'm sorry. I'm a new owner. I didn't know. I just didn't want to be late with my bill."

"Do you have a check you want to drop off?"

"Yes, but I need to write it out."

"I was just locking up. You'll have to come back another time." The man wore a dusty green trench coat.

"OK." Ruby leaned so she could see around him.

"What are you looking at?" he questioned her.

"It looks like you left a light on in the back, that's all."

He turned around. "Yeah, I'll get it."

Ruby had an overwhelmingly bad feeling about Anna Uchibori. She sensed she was in grave danger. She wondered, was she in the back room? Had she been tied up? Was she safe?

Ruby made her way down the steps quickly. She knew she needed to get to a phone, but something told her to find GamePlan and just make sure he was OK. She ran quickly to the paddock. The lights were still on at the stables. She walked down the corridor of the second building of stables where she remembered seeing his name on the stall door. She found it easily, as he was hanging his head out above the gate. She held her hand up and patted him on the neck.

"You're a good boy." She was amazed at how majestic he was. He did not flinch once when she touched him. "I'm going to make sure you are safe."

"May I help you?" She heard a Hispanic man's voice behind her and turned to see who it was. She had never seen the man before.

"You must be Ruby Sans." The man with leathery hands put one hand out to shake Ruby's. He held a rake in the other. "I'm Stan. I'm a groomer here."

"It's nice to meet you." She shook his hand. She wanted to tell him about her odd encounter with the man in the association office.

"I was here to see—"

"Anna, right?"

"Yes, how did you know?"

"She told me you would be coming."

"But she wasn't at the association office. There was a man there."

"Yes, she left the office."

"Ruby!" She heard Anna's voice behind her. She was so relieved to see her.

"Anna, I was so worried about you when I saw that man in the office."

"Yes, he's a bad guy. We need to get to work quickly before he might come down here to the stables."

"What do you mean he's a bad guy?" Ruby asked.

"Do you remember what I said that it is best to catch someone in the act?" Anna was good at answering questions with questions.

"Are you saying he is working with Kursta?"

"Why don't we be patient and see what unfolds?" Anna smiled at Ruby and Stan.

Anna opened the door to GP's stall and gently coaxed the horse to move so Ruby and Stan could enter. Anna pointed to a cabinet in the stall that held tack with a tiny knothole in the wood. "Camera," she whispered. She pointed to the opposite corner, close to the ground. "Camera," she whispered.

Ruby nodded her head.

"We wait until the right time," Anna said.

Stan tapped Ruby on the shoulder. "Come with me. Let me show you something."

Stan led the women out of the stall and down the corridor to the backside where the staff's quarters were. There were rows of apartments that looked like a large two-story motel. He led them up the stairs and pulled some keys out of his pocket at the second apartment from the end on the second floor. He opened the door and with a smile, motioned the women to go in ahead of him.

"What's going on? I don't feel comfortable." Ruby looked at Anna.

"Relax and trust us. This is for GP." Anna patted Ruby on the back. Ruby walked into the room, which looked much like a motel room until the three of them were inside and Stan closed the door. On the wall behind the door was a desk with two large monitors.

Stan pulled out the desk chair and sat down. The women watched without a word as he booted up the computer and proceeded to bring up four screens, two on each monitor. On two of the screens, they could see views of GP. He had his head out of his stall and was whinnying. Those clearly were from the cameras in the cabinet and on the floor. On the other monitors, you could see the corridor outside GP's stable and the view coming into the stable building from the entrance.

"You've done a lot of work," Ruby said.

"Like I said," Anna patted Ruby on the back, "I take care of all the planning. Stan, here, did all the installation."

All of a sudden, the man from the association office walked into the corridor.

"That's the man I saw." Ruby sucked in her breath.

"That's Sandy." Stan shook his head. "They call him the Sandman."

The thuggish-looking man went up to GP and held his hand out to him. GP snorted and went back inside his stall. From the inside cameras, you could see Sandy entering the stall.

"What is he going to do?" Ruby raised her voice. "Let's go get him."

"Not so fast," Anna motioned. "Hit record, Stan."

Stan pressed a button on the computer keyboard and started recording. Sandy started looking around the perimeter of the stall.

"What is he looking for?" Ruby questioned.

"An electrical outlet," Anna responded.

Sandy found one in the corner close to the camera. He bent down to inspect the socket, providing an extreme close-up of his left eyeball and cheek.

"What if he sees the camera?" Ruby had chills on her arms.

He must not have discovered it, as he backed away and left the stall.

"Why was he looking for an outlet?" Ruby asked.

"Time will tell," Anna said.

"That's not an acceptable answer." Ruby crossed her arms. "What is he going to do?"

"Stan here is watching over GP all day, all night. Don't worry. You can trust him."

"Where was he when the two other horses died? How do I know the same thing won't happen to GP?"

"Who do you think you can trust, Ms. Sans? It is true that the other two horses could not be saved. We were not able to get the cameras installed in time, but your horse will be watched twenty-four seven. Remember the pattern? Your horse has a race in three days."

"Why would Sandy be snooping around GP's stall when he hasn't even run the race yet? How does he know he's not going to win?"

Chapter 28

After his visit to the Green Gable Estate, Travis wasted no time getting the necessary supplies to start the restoration of the black carousel horse. He consulted with Jose at the antique store and was able to meet with a professional carousel maker. The restoration of this horse was going to be his gift to his newfound sister.

Ruby had given him the key to the garage and to the house and told him to make himself at home. The first thing he was going to do was completely wipe down the head and body. It took several cloths to do this. It was very filthy, and getting into the grooves of the mane on the head and the tail took a lot of time.

Travis took a cloth to the inside of the body. The first swipe brought out a couple of Daddy Long Legs that had made their home in the darkness. Upon the second swipe he heard the crumple of paper. He pulled out his cloth and looked deeper inside the wooden cavity. There was a paper caught up in the corner. He pulled it out.

It read, Certificate of Ownership and Authenticity.

Travis went into the house to call Ruby at the hotel. He hoped she would pick up. She was difficult to track down.

"Hello?"

"Hey, it's Travis. I wanted to let you know that I found a Certificate of Ownership and Authenticity document inside the Carousel Horse, of all places. It shows a picture of what appears to be a diamond. It sort of looks like a map with arrows pointing to different parts and angles on it. It has Hildegard's name on it."

"I can't even tell you how happy I am that you called!" Ruby almost squealed.

"I'm sorry to say that I didn't find the diamond to go with it."

"That's OK. Does it say anything else?" Ruby asked.

"It looks like it has a name, but it's hard to make out." There was a pause. "OK It looks like Canari Vert. I'm no francophone, but I think that would be French for Green Canary."

"That's the best news I've had all day. On another topic, how would you like to go to a horse race with me tomorrow?"

"I've never been to one before, but sure, why not?"

"Meet me in the hotel lobby at eleven a.m. Bring the certificate with you."

Chapter 29

As soon as Ruby hung up with Travis, she called the police station and asked for Detective Niver. Surprisingly, he was there.

"I need to talk to you about information I found on the diamond that Sydney Tracey found." Ruby walked as far as the phone cord in her hotel room would allow. How tired she was of living in that room!

"You mean the one that she stole?" he sneered. "Come on down to the station. Your timing couldn't be better."

Ruby wondered what he meant by that. She got in her car and arrived in less than ten minutes. She loved how quickly she was able to get around in downtown Tolstoy.

As she entered the building, she ran into Owen, who was coming out. He didn't look happy.

"What are you doing here?" Ruby's heart sped up, wondering if there was a new development in the case.

"Probably the same thing you're about to do," he said flatly.

"Do they have new evidence?" She could tell there was something gravely troubling him. He was much different than the last time she had seen him at the hotel bar. "Are you OK?" She studied his face, searching for any inkling of what may have transpired between him and the detectives before she walked into the station. She figured they wouldn't have released him if he was implicated, but his mood did not reflect that of a man who was free and clear.

He ignored all of her questions. "Did they call you in?"

"We've been trading messages. I just happened to catch Niver on the phone and he said now was a good time to come in."

"Do you mind if I go back with you? There's something I'd like to be around for when they tell you."

Ruby had no idea what he was talking about. "Why don't you just tell me yourself, then, now?"

"I want the detectives to be present."

"OK. As long as Niver and Mellon don't care, I'm fine with it."

Ruby walked up to the counter with Owen behind her.

"I'll buzz you in." The clerk recognized them.

Niver and Mellon were waiting for Ruby.

"You're back?" Mellon asked Owen.

"I really want to be in the room when she finds out."

Ruby looked at Owen, but he did not return eye contact as they followed the detectives into a small room with a table and four chairs. No observatory window in this room. Ruby and Owen sat with their backs to the door.

"OK, so what's going on?" Ruby looked around at the three men who all knew something she didn't. It was a matter of who was going to speak up first.

Detective Niver spoke first. "You and Mr. Kierney here have officially been cleared in the homicide case of Suki Giles."

Ruby wasn't sure what that meant exactly since she knew she never had anything to do with Suki's death in the first place. She also highly doubted that Owen was involved since they were together that night. She assumed they were about to tell her they solved the case.

"Excuse me if I don't jump for joy. Tell me something I don't already know. Do you know who killed Suki?"

"We have more information now, thanks to Mr. Kierney here."

In surprise, Ruby turned to get a clear view of Owen's face.

He still did not make direct eye contact with her, but

instead spoke in her direction. "You know that black Ford truck that was parked outside your house that night that I told you about?"

Ruby vividly remembered the conversation. "Yes, I remember you telling me about it. Obviously, I have no recollection of that night." Ruby shifted in her seat, a little uncomfortable that the detectives knew she had passed out that night.

"I know who it belongs to. His name is Sandy Gilman. He hangs out at the track." He finally turned to make full eye contact with her.

"Wait a second," Ruby said. "Sandy... Is he a big guy with bushy blond hair?"

"That would be him," Owen said.

"So, did he kill her?" Ruby sucked in her breath, thinking of him holding Suki down in the water.

"We are still piecing together the events of that night," Mellon explained. "We did find his fingerprints on many things in the house—on drawers and door handles, including the bathroom door—both on the outside and inside."

"We have reason to believe that if he did it, that he did not act alone," Niver continued. "While we cannot disclose any of the details yet, we think we should have the case cracked soon."

Ruby took a deep breath.

Niver continued, "We need your cooperation. We are not making any announcement that he is a suspect. Again, we cannot disclose any more than what we've told you. If you see him at the racetrack or any other place, you should steer clear of him. Do you understand?"

Ruby glanced over at Owen, who now did not seem afraid to look her in the eye. "Yes, I understand." She paused. "If we are finished with this topic, do you mind if I speak with the two of you privately?" Ruby turned her attention to the officers.

Owen took that as his cue to leave and stood up. "Well,

I guess I'll see you all later." He opened the door and paused to look at Ruby before exiting the room.

"There are actually two things I need to discuss with you," Ruby started. "First of all, I know more about Sandy Gilman, but I didn't want to talk about him in front of Mr. Kierney."

"Go on," prompted Mellon. Both officers seemed intent on knowing what Ruby would say next.

"When I inherited the fifty percent share in the racehorse from my aunt, I wasn't sure if I should keep it. Mr. Kierney, the horse's trainer and manager, tried to convince me the horse was running hot, that he was on a winning streak. The jockey, Roman Drewster, told me how well the horse had taken care of him; which I found odd, as he rides many horses, not just my horse. However, in reviewing the contracts between them and my aunt, I understand why they would want me to keep the horse and why they would want to keep their contract. My aunt and I have paid a disproportionate amount of their income. My co-owner, Kursta Blithey, doesn't pay a quarter of what my aunt paid them every month."

"I'm lost," Niver said, chewing a wad of gum. "What does this have to do with Sandy Gilman?"

"I'm getting there. So, while I was researching my horse's—Game Plan's—track record, I found that his hot streak had gone cold. In his prime, he did win a fair number of races, but he suffered a series of losses. There was a woman at the racing association office that—"

A knock on the door disrupted them. Someone opened the door.

"Come on in, Agent," Mellon motioned.

Ruby wondered what or who could be so important to interrupt her story. She turned around to see Anna Uchibori standing before her, blinking hard several times.

"Anna Uchibori, you're Agent Uchibori?"

Niver pulled an extra chair against the wall to the table so that Anna, Agent Uchibori, could sit with them.

"Do you trust me now?" Anna asked Ruby with a wide grin.

"What's going on? I assume Sandy Gilman is a suspect in Suki Giles' murder?"

"We'll get to that. Go on, you were in the middle of an important story before I came in. Don't let me interrupt you," Anna said.

Although she wouldn't be surprised if Anna had mind reading super powers, Ruby spotted a camera she hadn't noticed before in one of the upper corners of the room, reminding her of the ones Anna and Stan had pointed out to her in GP's stall at Diamond Head.

She had to take a moment to find where she'd left off. "So, I don't fault Owen or Roman for wanting to make a living. Have they been taking my aunt and me to the cleaners in horse fees? Maybe, but it's not illegal. Did they lead me to believe GamePlan was racing better than he actually was? Absolutely. Is that illegal? No. Is it unethical? In my book, yes; but again, it's not criminal. It's my responsibility to know my horse's track record."

"You did your homework. A-plus." Anna gave Ruby an approving smile and nodded her head.

Ruby continued, "In doing some deeper investigation, however—and thank you, Anna, for lighting my path—I came to see some similarities in the horses that died this month and my own GP. There is a pattern..."

The phone rang. Mellon answered it and handed the receiver to Anna.

"Yes?" She listened intently to the caller for half a minute. "We're on our way." She hung up the phone and blinked several times. "Ruby, the pattern's been broken," Anna said calmly before turning to the officers. "We've got to get to the track right away. They're setting up tonight."

Chapter 30

The three officers stood up and exited the room quickly, leaving Ruby behind. "What am I supposed to do?" she called after them. She thought for a moment and decided she would follow them. They hadn't said she couldn't.

Ruby's heart began to pound as she ran out of the police station to her car. There were so many thoughts swirling around in her head. She prayed that nothing had happened to her GP as she turned the key in the ignition. She wondered how Sandy Gilman was the link between the horse deaths and Suki's murder as she pulled out of the parking lot.

When Ruby arrived at the service gate, the closest one to the paddock and stalls, she didn't know that the electricity to all the gates surrounding the track complex perimeter had been disconnected. While Ruby struggled to get through the service gate, the detectives were challenged getting through the main entrance gate. They had also dispatched two marked cop cars that were trying to get through the back entrance, used mostly by VIPs. One by one, they all discovered they were going to have to climb the fence or squeeze through the gate and run to the stalls. Hopefully, Stan could keep things under control until reinforcements arrived.

Ruby got out of her car with the headlights still shining so she could see where she was running. She decided climbing over the service gate would be her easiest option, but she scraped her leg in the process. As she jumped to the ground, she could feel the beginning of a trickle of blood running down her ankle. She ran as fast as she could toward the paddock area. Up ahead, she saw two uniformed police officers with Anna, Niver, and Mellon trailing behind. She worked hard to catch up to them, but they were way ahead of her.

As she reached the paddock area, she heard voices yelling and something hitting on the walls. She was afraid of what she would find when she got to GP's stall.

"Freeze!" she heard a man's voice command firmly as she rounded the corner to GP's stall. It was Stan. He stood at the opening of the stall, blocking the view inside. His tan shirt was drawn tight, showing the lat muscles in his back. His arms were stretched out in front of him. Although she couldn't see it, she knew he was holding a handgun. Anna, Niver, Mellon, and the two uniformed officers all had their guns drawn behind him, pointing in the same direction of the open stall. Ruby couldn't see who they were pointed at. She was distracted momentarily by a large bloodstain on her white Converse shoe.

Stan disappeared into the stall now with the other cops behind him. Ruby still could not see inside. Clearly, there would have been no room for GP. Where had he gone?

There was a commotion. Someone was tackled to the ground. A few moments later, Stan could be heard from the stall. "You are hereby arrested for the equine deaths of Freakshot and Malfeasance, as well as the homicide of Suki Giles. You have the right to remain silent. Anything you say can and will be used against you in a court of law..." Sandy emerged from GP's stall in handcuffs, escorted by the two uniformed cops. His hair was adorned with hay. A moment later, Kursta Blithey emerged from the stall, also in handcuffs, and escorted by detectives Niver and Mellon. Stan followed them. Kursta made eye contact with Ruby and then looked at the ground, obviously ashamed.

Ruby heard Anna call her name from within the stall. "Come here." Ruby found Anna alone in the corner of GP's stall. GP was nowhere to be found.

"Where is GP? Is he OK?" Ruby was frantic.

"Trust me. GP is fine. I will show you to him in just a moment." At Anna's feet lay a briefcase.

"What's that?" Ruby asked.

"Do you remember when you questioned why Sandy was looking for an outlet when we were watching him on the camera in Stan's apartment?"

"Yes," Ruby recalled.

"This is how a horse can be killed without nearly any detection." Anna opened up the briefcase to reveal an extension cord that had been sliced down the middle. Alligator clips had been connected to the exposed wires. Anna held a clip with the wire attached in each hand. "One goes on the horse's ear; the other, on the rectum. Then, they plug it in and stand back. It is very difficult to detect foul play in this type of case. Sometimes there is a small singe mark where the clips have been placed."

The thought was so gruesome to Ruby she thought she might throw up on the spot. "I need to see GP. I need to know he is OK." Anna led Ruby out of the stall just as Owen Kierney was walking toward them with GamePlan on a lead.

"Here's your horse, safe and sound." Owen gave the lead to Ruby. She stroked GamePlan's neck, relieved he was unharmed.

"Owen Kierney is a brave man." Anna was talking to Ruby but she was looking at Owen. "He did the right thing in turning his mother in."

Ruby found a new respect for Owen. "Now I understand what you meant in the hotel when you said you do the right thing even when it's difficult. You knew your mom was involved then, didn't you?"

"I had a pretty good idea."

"How did you know?" Ruby asked.

"I went over to my mom's condo one day after she had met you at the horse track. She told me that she had been over to Mil's house and saw the diamonds on the desk in his office along with your Aunt Hilde's will. She said it almost caught on fire from the desk lamp. Anyway, she found out from Mil that you were Hilde's sole heir, and then knew you would have the diamonds. She asked me if I could get close to you and find out where the diamonds were. If I could get just one of them from you, she could sell it on the black market and split the profits with me. Then she could pay off Sandy." His green eyes locked with Ruby's. "But I would never do that. I told her I couldn't help her. She was in too deep with her bad financial decisions, and I wasn't going to bail her out."

"Why did she need to pay off Sandy?" Ruby clung to Owen's every word.

"My mom took out insurance policies on every horse she owned. That's not unusual or illegal. Many horse owners do. However, with some probing, she confessed to me that she had paid Sandy to put Kingston down."

"Hilde loved that horse!" Ruby cried.

"I know she did." Owen put his hand on Ruby's shoulder. "It's such a tragedy. She told me since the insurance company refused to pay on Kingston, which was supposed to be a one hundred fifty thousand dollar claim, she had no way of paying Sandy the fifty thousand she owed him for doing the dirty deed. Sandy had threatened to kill her if she didn't come up with the money within two weeks. She was a desperate wreck. I told her I didn't have that kind of money and wouldn't give it to her even if I did."

GP was getting restless. He turned his head from side to side, signaling he was ready to move. Owen patted him on the neck.

"She told me she asked Morgan for a loan, but he wouldn't give it to her because she refused to tell him why she needed it. She was afraid he would turn her in to the police himself if he knew she had committed insurance fraud."

GP raised one of his front legs and shook his head.

"I know, Boy." Owen patted GP on the neck. "Here, let's get him back to his stall."

Anna went before them and removed the Briefcase of Death. Owen kicked around the straw to make sure there were no lingering parts or anything else that could harm GP. He then led the horse into the stable and got him settled in for the night.

With the death suitcase in hand, Anna turned to Owen and Ruby. "I know the two of you have much more to talk about, but we need you to go back to the station to make final statements now."

Chapter 31

Ruby found her car just as she had left it, with the lights shining on the gate. She was relieved the battery wasn't dead. She climbed the gate, taking extra care not to injure herself this time.

As she drove back to the station, the many unanswered questions about Suki's murder and horse deaths flooded her. She also remembered that she had the opportunity to tell Niver and Mellon about the Green Canary's Certificate of Authenticity that Travis had found. As far as she knew, Sydney was still in jail and would need that document with Hilde's name on it along with Hilde's will to prove that the diamond now rightly belonged to Ruby. Hopefully then, any charges against Sydney Tracey could be dropped.

Once at the station, the clerk barely made eye contact with Ruby as she buzzed her in and piped, "Last door on the end."

Everyone was back in the large room with the window—Niver and Mellon, Stan and Anna, the two uniformed officers, and Owen. Ruby was the last one to the party.

"Would you like some coffee?" Anna offered as Ruby proceeded to pull up a chair at the table in the middle of the room.

Ruby shook her head no and said thanks as she seated herself next to Owen. "Can someone please finally tell me exactly who killed my best friend and why?"

The group became silent and everyone looked at her. The two uniformed officers excused themselves from the room.

Officer Mellon, seated directly across from Ruby, scooted his chair closer to the table. "When Sandy put pressure on Kursta to come up with a plan to pay him off, she felt she had no choice but to take him to your house in hopes that the diamonds would be there. She knew you would be at the race association party with her son, Mr. Kierney. She thought they could get in, find the diamonds—or at least one of them—and get out."

Niver picked up the story from there. "What they weren't counting on was for someone else to be in the house. Apparently, your roommate was in the bathroom taking a bath. They heard her call out as they were in the middle of going through drawers and cabinets. She proceeded to get out of the tub, but before she could, Mr. Gilman pushed her under the water and strangled her."

Ruby started crying. She couldn't bear to think of what Suki had endured.

Anna stood up from her seat and went over to Ruby. She put her arms out to hug her. Anna held Ruby, allowing her to sob into her shoulder. Anna didn't have to bend over very far, even with Ruby in a sitting position.

"I am so very sorry for what happened to your friend." Anna released their embrace.

"Thank you."

Niver pushed a box of tissue sitting on the table closer to where Ruby could reach it and continued. "Kursta continued to search for the diamonds while Sandy..." his voice trailed off as he chose not to complete the sentence. "She only found one diamond. As you know, it was in the top dresser drawer in your bedroom."

Ruby recalled her careless thought process in leaving the diamond in that spot.

Detective Mellon added, "Once they had the diamond, they left the house through the back slider. Kursta stuffed the GIA study into the bushes as they left the back yard through the gate."

From there, the detectives took final statements from both Ruby and Owen.

"There was something I didn't get to speak to you about earlier," Ruby reminded Niver and Mellon as she got ready to leave. "I found the Certificate of Authenticity on the other diamond. My brother found it at my aunt's estate. Can I bring it to you tomorrow around noon along with my aunt's will?"

"That would be perfect." Detective Mellon shook Ruby's hand and patted her on the back.

Chapter 32

Ruby went back to the Hotel Meridien and crashed for what she hoped would be the last time. She planned to check out in the morning.

When she woke up, she remembered that she was to meet Travis at 11 a.m., not only to get the chameleon diamond certificate from him, but also to take him to GP's race. She and Owen had agreed the night before, as they walked to their respective cars after putting GP to bed, that it would be best to pull GP from the race. What Ruby hadn't told Owen, however, was that GP would never run another race.

Ruby attempted to call Travis a few times in the morning but was never able to catch him. She waited in the hotel lobby for him to show up. As expected, he was dressed up in what she was sure was his nicest outfit aside from his suit—a pair of black Dockers, a black button-up shirt, and a shiny blue tie. He wore black tennis shoes.

In contrast, Ruby wore her favorite comfy jeans and a green t-shirt. She wore her white Converse shoes from the night before, the bloodstain now a brown color. Admittedly, she needed to go shopping.

"I wore the blue tie because I know that's one of GP's colors and it's my only tie," Travis chuckled. "No offense, but you don't look like you're dressed up for a race."

"Yeah, about the race..." Ruby started explaining as Travis fished out the folded diamond certificate from his shirt pocket. "There's been a little change of plans. Why don't we have some brunch at the hotel? I have another proposition for you."

* * *

Ruby pulled the Certificate of Ownership and Authenticity out from her purse and handed it to Detective Mellon. Niver was off for the day.

"This was found in a carousel horse in my garage, which used to be my aunt's garage. I believe this is the document you need to prove that the diamond Sydney Tracey took in fact was part of my aunt's estate, which is now rightly mine."

Officer Mellon took a look at it. "We will give it to the analyst to compare the two. Do you have a copy of your aunt's will?"

Ruby fished in her purse for the document, which was beginning to show some wear with recent handling. She handed it over to the detective.

"Can she be released today?" Ruby thought it was a long shot, but one could hope, right?

"Doubtful. We need time to analyze the documents. Her court date is set for tomorrow." Mellon thumbed through the will.

"I thought she would have already had it."

"It's been delayed a few times. Once the analyst reviews the certificate and compares it to the diamond, if everything checks out, you'll have your other diamond back."

Ruby returned to the hotel and gathered up her belongings. She stuffed what she had in her little Karman Ghia and checked out at the front desk. She had some belongings from the Blue House, the name she had given to her former place with Suki, in a storage unit. She would get help from Travis in moving the rest of her stuff into the Green Gable Estate.

Chapter 33

Two weeks after Ruby permanently checked out of the Hotel Meridien, she was finally feeling like the Green Gable Estate was home. She gazed out the kitchen window to the expanse of the field that Travis had recently built a field fence around. Ruby watched him as he made an adjustment on the new gate. She finished washing her hands and went outside to meet him.

"You are a man of many talents, my brother." Ruby smiled at his accomplishment.

They both turned their heads to the direction of a vehicle coming up the drive. It was a white Chevy Silverado pickup pulling a sweet matching horse trailer. Travis and Ruby watched as the driver deftly maneuvered the horse trailer, backing it up to the gate Travis had just installed.

Owen Kierney hopped out of the driver's side.

"Hey, Ruby! I got your new addition in the back." He shook Travis' hand and the men introduced themselves to each other.

Ruby was giggly with excitement. She ran to the side of the horse trailer where GamePlan was showing his beautiful face.

Owen opened the back of the trailer and put down the ramp. Then he unhooked GP. He led him out and down the ramp into his new, large pasture. Travis closed the gate. Owen and Ruby both watched the horse explore his new home as if they were watching their baby.

"He's got a million-dollar view, doesn't he?" Owen

scanned the gorgeous view of the city in the distance below. He turned and smiled at Ruby. "You made the right decision."

"You really think so?" Tears of joy filled her eyes.

"No doubt in my mind." Owen pulled Ruby to him in a real embrace.

Chapter 34

"So, this is it, huh? Africa or bust?" Travis and Ruby stood looking at each other in the loading zone at the airport.

"Don't worry, Bro. I'll be back in three months."

"Three months is a long time." He kicked at her shoe, playfully.

"I know, but you'll be fine. You'll have GP and the creepy orange cat to keep you company, if it ever comes back around."

"We'll miss you."

"And I'll miss you." She gave her brother an extra tight squeeze.

"I should have the carousel horse done by the time you get back."

"I can't wait."

Ruby waved to Travis and then turned to enter the airport terminal with her large hound's-tooth-print roller suitcase in tow. She patted her purse holding the African map along with the pillbox holding the seven pins. She was keeping the promise she'd made to herself.

The End

~

Kelley Sewell, a northern California native, grew up spending summers camping at nearby lakes and taking trips with her family to national parks across the country. An outdoor and travel enthusiast, she enjoys hiking and visiting new places. Kelley holds an English degree from UCLA and is a member of Sisters in Crime and Writers Forum, a nonprofit organization for writers in Northern California. She lives with her husband and two sons. **kelleysewell.com**

~

Proof

Made in the USA
Columbia, SC
15 April 2018